OTHER YEARLING BOOKS YOU WILL ENJOY:

THE SECRET IN MIRANDA'S CLOSET, *Sheila Greenwald*
ALL THE WAY TO WIT'S END, *Sheila Greenwald*
VALENTINE ROSY, *Sheila Greenwald*
GIVE US A GREAT BIG SMILE, ROSY COLE, *Sheila Greenwald*
IT ALL BEGAN WITH JANE EYRE, *Sheila Greenwald*
THE MARIAH DELANY LENDING LIBRARY DISASTER, *Sheila Greenwald*
WILL THE REAL GERTRUDE HOLLINGS PLEASE STAND UP?,
Sheila Greenwald
THE AGONY OF ALICE, *Phyllis Reynolds Naylor*
AND MAGGIE MAKES THREE, *Phyllis Reynolds Naylor*
MAGGIE TOO, *Phyllis Reynolds Naylor*

YEARLING BOOKS/YOUNG YEARLINGS/YEARLING CLASSICS are designed especially to entertain and enlighten young people. Patricia Reilly Giff, consultant to this series, received the bachelor's degree from Marymount College. She holds the master's degree in history from St. John's University, and a Professional Diploma in Reading from Hofstra University. She was a teacher and reading consultant for many years, and is the author of numerous books for young readers.

For a complete listing of all Yearling titles,
write to Dell Readers Service,
P.O. Box 1045, South Holland, IL 60473.

The Atrocious Two

WRITTEN AND ILLUSTRATED BY
Sheila Greenwald

A Yearling Book

Published by
Dell Publishing
a division of
The Bantam Doubleday Dell Publishing Group, Inc.
666 Fifth Avenue
New York, New York 10103

The trademark Yearling® is registered in the U.S. Patent and Trademark Office.

ISBN: 0-440-40141-0

Printed in the United States of America

February 1989

10 9 8 7 6 5 4 3 2

CW

to Harriet Wasserman

Chapter
1

Cecilia took a deep breath. The only problem with hiding in the broom closet was the way the air got used up. It was very stuffy. However, this problem was far outweighed by the advantages, one of which was overhearing juicy conversations like the one she was now listening to. She mopped her damp brow and pushed her eye closer to the crack.

Cecilia had just known in her bones when she woke up that morning that this would be a good breakfast to spy on. She had stepped in among the brooms only minutes before her mother, yawning and blinking, had arrived to put the kettle on.

Tom and Julia Melton lived with their children, Ashley, aged eleven, and Cecilia, aged ten, in an

enormous and beautifully furnished apartment in an equally beautiful building that faced Central Park. It was in the white- and cocoa-colored kitchen of this apartment one sunny morning in early April that Cecilia, hiding in the broom closet just off the butler's pantry, overheard Tom Melton say to Julia Melton,

"What are we going to do with the children this summer?"

Through the slightly opened door of the broom closet Cecilia watched her mother look up from the *Times* and frown over her coffee cup. "Oh dear," she said.

"What about that camp they went to last summer?" asked Tom.

Julia shook her pretty head sorrowfully. "The directors wrote to say please not to think of sending Cecilia and Ashley back, because they won't take them. They were very hard to handle."

Cecilia saw her father's face sag.

"There are plenty of other camps, my dear," Julia said brightly, "and to one of them they shall surely go." She took a sip of coffee, sighed, and grew thoughtful. "But my problem is not July and August; it's June, awful June. That month between school and summer camp. I've got to go to Paris for the shows and then work like a horse on my resort line." Julia was a very successful fashion designer. Tom wrote TV shows.

"Do you think your Aunt Cynthia would like to take them for the month of June?" asked Tom. Then he remembered something. "I believe they've matured since last time."

"Last time." Julia shuddered. "Cynthia flew them home one day after they arrived. San Francisco is not around the corner."

"Yes, I remember now. She felt awful about it. Said she had no idea what a handful they'd be."

"And how old she had become."

"Cynthia doesn't understand modern children, does she," said Tom.

"How could she, Tom? She doesn't see children much and never had any of her own. It's been years since *I* spent summers with Aunt Cynthia and Aunt Tessie. I doubt Cynthia's taken a child since. It's too bad. They were wonderful summers." Julia smiled at the recollection. "What terrific old girls they were. What fun we had."

"What ever happened to the other one? To Tessie?" Tom asked.

"She was the eccentric one. She took a job on an Indian reservation near Santa Fe, got married to somebody called Flowers, taught school there, ran a shop — always doing something different. I've lost track of her. The last I heard was from Cynthia, who wrote to say that Tessie had bought a big place at Upton Manor in Connecticut. Tessie would never think of writing herself."

"Peculiar as all get-out," Tom concluded, "and not available to take the kids."

Julia shook her head from side to side. "No, Tom. Not Cynthia, not Tessie, not your sister, or my brother or either set of our parents. Not any of them."

"Not any of them," Tom echoed. Both Meltons reflected silently on the growing list of people who, with the same excuses, had returned Cecilia and Ashley after drastically shortened visits: "Too hard to handle," and "Had an awful effect on our own children. Susan wept in her room and wouldn't come out till Cecilia was gone," and "Love to see you two but PLEASE DON'T BRING THE CHILDREN."

The fact of it was, as Cecilia and Ashley knew very well, Tom and Julia were forever trying to get rid of them. They also knew why. Cecilia and Ashley did not need to eavesdrop to learn that they were atrocious. They knew quite well that they were. Whenever they had a choice to behave or not to behave themselves, they chose *not*. Their parents' reluctance to take them on trips was no surprise to them.

The broom closet had become unbearably stuffy and her parents' conversation seemed to have come to a depressing halt, so Cecilia eased herself out into the pantry and thence softly back down the hall toward her bedroom. She passed Ashley's room and heard a thumping sound. Ashley was lying on his bed, bounc-

5

ing a ball off a Beatrix Potter poster of Jemima Pud-
dleduck.

"Guess what, Ash," Cecilia said as she burst in.
"They're figuring out where to dump us again."

"There's nobody left!" Ashley hooted.

"Not quite," said Cecilia, drawing out her moment. She adored knowing something Ashley didn't.

Ashley threw the ball into the corner and sat up,
leaning on one elbow. "What's up?"

"There's another great-aunt. She's called Tessie
Flowers, she's Cynthia's sister, and she's eccentric."
Cecilia paused. "Whatever that is."

"Crazy, I think."

"Anyway, she's peculiar too, and I think Julia's
going to track her down for us. You know Julia when
she's desperate."

Ashley got off his bed. His brow was furrowed in
deep thought. Whenever he was thinking he did
some active physical thing, like running or walking or
throwing balls. Then softly he said to Cecilia, "Why
don't they take us for once? Why don't they just pack
us up and take us to Paris or California or something
instead of, you know . . ."

"Getting rid of us," Cecilia provided. Then she
had a brainstorm. "Hey, Ash, let's ask them. Let's.
Let's tell them that our friends, the kids we know, get

6

to go along sometimes. Janie Evans once went to Arizona, and Sandy went to Mexico. Maybe they never thought of it."

This idea sent Cecilia and Ashley bounding down the hall to the kitchen, where Tom and Julia looked up from their newspapers and coffee with expressions of alarm.

"Cecilia says you're trying to find out where to dump us again," Ashley began.

"And it's not easy," Cecilia said.

"Whatever is this about, my darlings?" Julia was flustered and wide-eyed. "Who ever said a word about it?"

"You did, this morning," Cecilia said, "and nobody will take us anymore, and Ashley's got a super idea, so listen."

Tom and Julia both overcame their embarrassment. They were very eager to hear Ashley's idea.

"You can make arrangements for us for June and July and August, and we'll be perfectly behaved. We swear on everything and we promise," Ashley said. He was getting more and more excited.

"We'll be model children, not atrocious," Cecilia put in.

"Oh, my goodness, what wonderful plan is this?" Julia clapped her hands.

"Something really brilliant. Something that you never thought of but is right under your nose," said Ashley.

"Tell us," said Tom. "I can't stand the suspense."

"TAKE US WITH YOU," said Ashley.

Julia and Tom seemed to go out like light bulbs. They not only dimmed; they deflated and looked horrified. Horrified and scared.

"Oh, dear, me, no," Julia said. "That would simply never work. You see, we shall both be so frightfully busy with meetings and shows, morning noon and night, that we would have no time at all to be with you. You would be bored to tears, and we all know too well what happens when you are even slightly bored. I think I don't need to go into that."

Tom nodded vehemently. "You know how nervous we get when we're repeatedly interrupted by your demands. It would be impossible for us to do a lick of work."

Yes, they knew, and had been told often enough that Tom and Julia could not do a blessed thing when exposed to the chaos and noise Cecilia and Ashley made.

"It would *never* work," Julia concluded.

"Okay." Ashley turned on his heel and went back to his room, with an odd cold smile on his lips.

"Okay." Cecilia said after him, and then she tore over to the refrigerator and opened it and in her loudest, most unpleasant, growl said, "You never have anything I like."

"Daddy will give you money so that you can pick up something you like on the way to school."

"M and M's and chips." Cecilia whipped around. "I'll get a big M and M's and chips."

"It's so bad for your teeth," Julia remarked vaguely, "and it's all you ever eat. Lord knows I've tried to get real food into you, but I'd probably have to make such a project my life's work. You're old enough to give me some cooperation, Cecilia."

"M and M's don't melt in your hand," Cecilia pointed out while helping herself to a spoonful of jam.

"Just all over your poor rotting little teeth," Tom said.

Cecilia threw the spoonful of jam in his direction and stamped her foot. "I like M and M's, and M and M's are my FOOD. I love them." Her gravelly voice worked up to a raucous shout, something like crying, but there were no tears. "They're my favorite thing to eat, and if you don't let me eat my M and M's I'll never eat anything else again in my WHOLE LIFE."

Julia and Tom looked at each other in dismay.

Cecilia's round tough face was creasing into the

ominous grimace that preceded one of her fits. She bared her small teeth. The doorbell rang, to the Meltons' relief. Cecilia stopped in mid-fit and ran off to open it.

"Thank God, it's Ulrika," said Tom. "I thought she'd never come."

Both Meltons seemed enormously relieved that Ulrika, the housekeeper, had arrived, and they could dress and go to work. However, it was not Ulrika whom Cecilia led into the kitchen. It was the building's superintendent, Mr. Pelch. He looked upset and embarrassed.

"Mr. Pelch, what can I do for you?" Julia asked apprehensively.

"You can tell Ashley to stop throwing wet toilet paper out the window. There's lots of complaints."

"Oh, God." Tom rose quickly and dashed down the hall toward his son's bedroom. "Ashley," he yelled, "stop it." He opened the door as Ashley, leaning on the windowsill, turned a blank pink face from the window. In his hand was a wad of wet toilet paper.

"Stop that this instant," Tom said sharply. "This instant."

Very slowly Ashley turned back toward the window to consider what his father had requested. A gentleman in a tan fedora was at that very moment walking beneath his window. The temptation was overwhelming, and he turned back to his father only after letting the paper fly. "Stop what, Dad?"

"That," said Tom.

"Oh, okay." Out of paper anyway, Ashley closed the window.

The doorbell rang again, and this time it was Ulrika. The Meltons never kept housekeepers for long. They had given up trying to hire someone to sleep in. Ulrika was only two weeks on the job and was already showing the familiar signs of sullenness and rage. Cecilia and Ashley were still sizing her up. They watched her carefully as she removed her hat and coat.

"I'm so glad you're here, Ulrika dear," Julia said, after she had ushered Mr. Pelch out the door. "Mr. Melton and I will be dining out tonight, so I want to leave you a list of groceries to buy and tell you what to prepare for the children's dinner."

"M and M's," said Cecilia. "I want M and M's and a Coke."

"Hush, darling."

"Ennnn-hennnn" Cecilia whinnied.

"Ulrika will make you something yummy."

"I hate her food," said Cecilia. "She cooks kaka and peepee and poopoo."

"Stop it, now," Julia pleaded.

Ulrika reddened and turned her bland fat face toward Cecilia. "I cook good stuff."

"Poopoo kaka peepee."

"Please, darling, stop it this minute or Ulrika will be very distressed with you and won't love you anymore."

Ulrika's lip curled in an expression that implied that she had never loved Cecilia to start with and that she was restraining herself with great effort from letting Cecilia know just how much she had come not to love her. At that moment Ashley came in and grabbed Cecilia by the arm.

"I have to tell you something." He pulled her with him down the hall to his room.

Once in his room, Ashley slammed the door and leaned against it. "We'll call her up," he said.

"Who?" Cecilia was mystified.

"The peculiar aunt they're trying to dump us on."

"They don't know where she is."

"You said you heard."

"Upton Manor, Connecticut, Julia said, but no address. Just Tessie Flowers."

"We have enough to get the number from Information."

"What will we say?"

"That we're calling for Mrs. Melton and will Tessie Flowers call Julia Melton, collect, in five minutes."

"Then what do we do?" Cecilia didn't quite get the idea, though she could see that Ashley was hatching something big.

"Then we do to her what we did to Cynthia and all the others, only we do it worse so that she ships us out and we come home and Tom and Julia have no place else to send us."

"And they have to take us along with them," Cecilia said in a flash. Now she saw the whole picture. Sometimes her dumb brother showed signs of pure genius. They had a much better chance of being shipped out immediately from Tessie's house than from a camp. Camps tended to keep one all summer, no matter what.

They didn't even have to leave Ashley's room to phone Information in Connecticut. He had a red wall phone hanging over his bed.

"Information for Upton Manor, please," said Ashley in his most polite voice. Then, while Cecilia rocked on the bed clutching her sides with stifled hilarity, he used his most grown-up disguise voice to say "Mrs. Tessie Flowers, a message from Julia Melton. Would you please call her, collect, in five minutes at the following number. She wishes to speak with you on urgent business." Ashley gave the number and hung up quickly, before Tessie had a chance to ask any questions.

After he had hung up Ashley joined Cecilia, laughing and rocking, on the bed.

He had hatched a scheme, true enough, but not

in their wildest or most mischievous daydreams could Ashley and Cecilia have known where this phone call would lead them and how it would change their lives forever after.

When the telephone rang exactly five minutes later, Ashley and Cecilia were waiting in the kitchen. Ashley wrenched the phone from its cradle. "Who is it?" he barked.

Julia came in. "Who is it?" she asked.

"Tessie who? I don't know you." Ashley handed the phone to Julia. "For you."

"Tessie?" Julia cried. "This is a miracle. You won't believe it, but Tom and I were just wondering about you." She stopped speaking and listened, a puzzled expression on her face. "Urgent business? A message? Good heavens, it must have been my fairy godmother. The only urgent business we have right now is trying to find a place for the children to spend the month of June. Just this morning I was remembering the wonderful vacations I spent with you and Cynthia, and I thought of you and wondered if it wouldn't be a simply terrible inconvenience if we . . ." She petered out and listened and then exclaimed, "Tessie, darling, you angel, are you quite sure?" She listened again, growing pink with delight.

Cecilia and Ashley were careful not to look at each other.

"Tessie, you wonder. They'd be thrilled, and Tom and I would be so grateful. I have to be in Paris, and Tom's got a deadline for a new show and has to go to the Coast." After this, Julia and Tessie chatted for a few minutes, exchanging news of relatives and friends. Then Julia caught sight of the kitchen clock. "Tessie darling, I have to run. "I'll call very soon to discuss all these exciting plans and bring you up to date." When she hung up the phone Julia was radiant. "Tom," she called out, "you won't believe our luck."

Tom came in to the kitchen, dressed and curious.

"That was my Aunt Tessie. She wants the children to visit her in the country and she wants them for the entire summer, just as soon as they're out of school. She says she has a large place in Connecticut. She told me that she's heard all about the children from Cynthia and is longing to know them and is very eager to have young folks about her again. She asked if we would consider allowing her to borrow Cecilia and Ashley from June to early September."

Tom and Julia beamed at one another in unbelieving joy. All their prayers had been magically answered.

Chapter
2

And so it came to pass that on the first Monday of the second week in June, Ed Jones, the doorman, said to Mr. Pelch, "There they go." Both men watched a yellow cab pull out from the curb and down Fifth Avenue.

"The atrocious two," Mr. Pelch said. He scratched his head. "How did two nice people like Mr. and Mrs. Melton do it?"

Only twenty minutes later on the platform at Grand Central Station, standing with the children's baggage just outside the train door, Julia was saying, "Cecilia darling, please don't wipe your hands on that precious skirt. It would be a crime to ruin it with chocolate. I'd so like you to make a nice first impression on Aunt Tessie."

"I hate Aunt Tessie. I hate this dress." Cecilia wiped her chocolated hand on the skirt. "Oh look," she observed with surprise. "It *does* melt in your hand." Cecilia always looked frightful. She managed to ruin in no time at all the darling little ensembles Julia put her into. In minutes the blouse was out of the skirt, the buttons dangling, and the hems torn. All this came before stains and dirt, which soon followed. Her straight brown hair, no matter how carefully brushed, managed to pop every which way, and of course her cheeks and mouth were stained with whatever candy she happened to be cramming into her face at the time. Ashley, on the other hand, usually appeared neat and tidy and smiling. His was the surprise attack. Neat, tidy, and smiling, he hit people over the head, jumped them from behind, and threw things at them. Today he was positively shining with cleanliness and (for anyone who knew him well) alarming in his sweet, smiling, compliant attitude.

"You will remember that the stop is Upton Manor and Aunt Tessie will be right there to meet you and Daddy told the conductor to remind you and tell you at the stop before to get ready. Oh, do be good children and sweet and helpful and polite. Tessie is an old lady now."

Cecilia filled her cheeks with M & M's and flashed a grin.

"All aboard," said the conductor.

They all went into the train so that Tom and Julia could settle the children and their baggage and give them their bags of sandwiches and kiss them a last good-by and give them each a fresh dollar bill and make them promise to write soon. "Remember, it's Upton Manor," Julia said.

"Say, I get out at Upton," a kindly man said as he slid into the seat behind them. "Don't you worry a bit. I'll tell the children when to get off and I'll keep an eye on them."

"Thank you *so* much." Julia turned her prettiest smile on the man and extended her gloved hand. "I can't tell you how much I appreciate that."

The train lurched. Julia grabbed her purse, Tom took her arm, and they ran for the door. As the train pulled out, Julia and Tom waved and smiled, but Cecilia and Ashley never looked back.

"This is our greatest challenge," said Ashley. "We've got to get her to cry uncle by tomorrow. We should be back in the city by the day after tomorrow. Mom's plane leaves at seven P.M. and Dad's at eight. They won't have time to find a camp for us or to dump us anyplace else."

"They'll have to take us with them. I'll go to
Paris with Julia; you go to California with Tom."

"Suits me," Ashley said.

They were silent for a moment, thinking of what
they were about to do. "I really could behave and all
that if Julia took me," Cecilia said. "I can do it. I
know how. Even though I never practiced."

"So can I," Ashley said. "I could be just like
Jason Schultz."

Jason Schultz, the son of friends of the Meltons,

was a model boy, serious and well behaved. Julia and Tom always marveled at the Schultz boy's behavior and commented, "They can take him anywhere." After Julia said this Ashley and Cecilia would be aware of her large purple eyes falling sadly and questioningly on them, as if to say "Why can't I have children like that."

"What are we going to do at Tessie's?" asked Cecilia. "What's the plan of action?"

"We'll do what we did at Cynthia's, only more of it," Ashley said. He needed to say no more. Cecilia knew exactly how to proceed. "If she's really old she may send us back after dinner."

"I don't think there's a night train." Ashley was distracted, making bread balls from his sandwich which he shot with his thumb at the kindly man behind him.

For the rest of the train ride, Ashley and Cecilia lived up to their reputation. They were just rehearsing for what they planned to do at Tessie's. Cecilia barreled up and down the train aisle, flicking newspapers out of people's hands, smearing chocolate on whatever she touched, and stealing tickets out of their slots on the backs of the train seats. By the time the train pulled into Upton Manor, the Melton children had earned the label "atrocious" from some thirty-nine new victims, who heaved sighs of relief to see them depart at last. "Those are the worst kids I seen on the line in twenty years" was the way the conductor summed them up.

On the platform the nice man, who now had two of Ashley's bread bullets suspended in his thin gray hair, ran for his waiting car without a word. Cecilia and Ashley looked around curiously. The handful of people who had gotten off the train all seemed to know where they were going or whom they were meeting. Before long, they were all gone. Where was Aunt Tessie? The platform was empty. This was a situation they had not planned on. As they looked around them, a rusty, ancient car pulled into the small parking area near the tracks. Out of the car emerged an old woman. She had white frizzy hair all around her head, and she walked oddly. She was exceedingly bent to the right. As she approached them, they noticed two very blue unblinking eyes.

"Hello, you two." She waved. "Sorry I'm late. I'm your old Aunt Tessie."

Chapter
3

"I'll bet you kids are famished," Tessie said as they pulled out of the parking area.

Ashley and Cecilia were quiet, which was the way they always began.

"You had such a long trip up. Country air always makes people hungry." Tessie drove slowly down the town's main street for two blocks and then turned onto a narrower road. "Well, I've got a nice meal waiting for you."

"What is it?" said Cecilia.

Tessie was silent for a minute before answering. She stopped for a stop sign and, without turning, said, "Kaka peepee and poopoo. You know."

Ashley's smile froze.

"I don't like that," Cecilia said weakly.

"Too bad, because that's what I serve." Tessie was matter-of-fact. "My cooking is like Cynthia's, and she tells me that's what you decided her cooking was made of." Then she turned around to smile at them. "Cynthia told me all about the two of you. I know what I'm in for."

Ashley and Cecilia looked at the road they had turned down. It was dense with shrubbery and trees. They had no idea where they were. Cecilia's face crumpled. "Ennnn-hennnn," she whimpered.

"Can it." Tessie stepped on the accelerator. "Your mother was a fine little girl. A pleasure to have. She liked my cooking. I'm a first-rate cook. But if you don't like it here or if *I* don't like you, you

can walk back to New York. I have just enough gas to get us to the house." At this point they passed a gas station. Tessie honked her horn and waved to the attendant, who tipped his hat at her. "Hi, Al," she hollered.

"You could buy more gas," Cecilia pointed out. "Are you too poor?"

"Yes," Tessie said.

"Well, my father and my mother have lots of money," Cecilia informed her, "and all we have to do is call them up and they'll fly us anyplace on American Express, like California to New York or Europe, even."

"Only thing is," Tessie said slowly, "I won't let you use my phone."

"Then I'll write them a letter," Cecilia said. "I've got my own stamps." She leaned back in the seat and drew her knees up to her chin. Ashley winked at her. This kind of arguing was part of their strategy. It helped to wear the victim down.

"You're a very smart girl, Cecilia," Tessie said after a bit. "Very plucky and smart. I'm glad to see that. It will come in handy."

"What's that supposed to mean?" Ashley asked.

"You'll see. I've got plans for you kids." Tessie turned the car off the blacktop road onto a rocky dirt one so densely overhung that branches and twigs popped through the windows and snapped while they made their bumpy way.

As they traveled farther down this road, all the sass and pluck went out of Cecilia. For the first time, both Melton children experienced an ominous sensation that made them fall silent. At last they came to a clearing, and what they saw caused the greatest surprise they had known on this very surprising day. A large, almost huge, Victorian mansion loomed before them. Even to the inexperienced eyes of Cecilia and Ashley, it appeared to be a hopeless ruin. What few shingles were left dangled from the eaves, paint peeled in great curling sheets, windows filled with cardboard looked out like blind eyes. The approach to the house, a once grand drive bordered with majestic evergreens, was equally scraggly. Everything matched. Everything was in a state of ruin.

"This is it," Tessie said. "Home." She stopped the car halfway round the circular drive, directly in front of the veranda steps. "Okay, smarties. Take your bags and let's get going. I call this place Moby Dick." Though she was smiling, her blue eyes did not change expression. Cecilia and Ashley climbed out of the car and looked up the flight of broken steps to the high-columned veranda and the chipped and broken double doors through which they would pass.

The air smelled of damp and fresh grass and something else. There was a delicious cooking smell. The smell was the first comforting thing they had experienced since Aunt Tessie picked them up at the station. With suitcases in hand, Cecilia and Ashley followed Tessie up the stairs and through the door. To the left was a large, high-ceilinged living room, neat and comfortable, with stereo, sofa, easy chairs, and shelves of books. To the right was an empty (save for dining table) dining room, and before them a heavy mahogany staircase rising into shadows.

"Now, as you can see, we've been working our tails off since April to get these rooms nice," Tessie said. "Fresh paint, plaster, and scraped floorboards have worked miracles."

Miracles? Cecilia and Ashley looked at the tidy, humble rooms and thought Tessie must be out of her mind, or joking.

She did not smile or laugh, however. She was not joking. "Follow me, folks" was all she said as she headed up the staircase. They climbed one flight and walked down a corridor with uneven, warped floorboards, lined by closed doors. Tessie opened one of these doors on the left and one directly opposite on the right. "That one is yours, Cecilia, and that one is yours, Ashley." They looked first into Cecilia's room and then Ashley's. Both rooms were pleasant and tidy. Each contained a brass bedstead, a bureau with a mirror, a night table and night lamp, a standing closet and a chair. The windows looked out into the leaves of trees (tulip for Cecilia and willow for Ashley).

"Now get out of those silly clothes and come down to the kitchen when you're ready. You'll find the kitchen by following the smells of food. While we eat supper, I'll explain your work schedules, and we'll have a real fine time."

"Work schedules?" Cecilia and Ashley said together.

Tessie turned around and faced them. At last she blinked. "What do you think I asked you here for? To make mischief and drive me crazy? You two are going to help turn this dump into a respectable paying guest house." She went off to the kitchen.

Chapter
4

"We've got to get out of here, Ashley. What'll we do?" Cecilia rarely appealed to her brother, believing that she was a zillion times smarter than he and having made it her mission in life to convince him of this. Poor Ashley, who believed his sister was a zillion times smarter, couldn't get over her sudden collapse. He wanted to rise to her faith in him but couldn't think of a thing to say.

"I don't know," he mumbled.

"What do you mean, you don't know? You've got to know. You've got to come up with something. We can't stay here. She's horrible, maybe even crazy. Maybe she'll kill us."

Ashley and Cecilia had completely forgotten their original plan, the plan they had laid so confidently, down to the last detail, back in New York. At that time Tessie had been a paper-doll old lady. Now that they had met her, the world was upside down. It was no longer a question of getting back to New York in time to be taken along by Tom and Julia. It was now a question of survival.

"How can we make her give up? What did we do at Cynthia's?" Cecilia tried frantically to remember.

"The usual things," Ashley said. "But they won't work. Tessie is different."

Tessie called up from someplace downstairs. "What's keeping you two? Come on down. I'm waiting."

Cecilia went to her room and changed. Five minutes later she and Ashley and Aunt Tessie gathered in the kitchen.

"Now that's better." Tessie approved of the T-shirts and blue jeans. They stood facing each other in the large kitchen, which they had found with no trouble, in back of the dining room.

The kitchen was filled with the rich rosy light of late afternoon. It was also full of very old-fashioned things. Old refrigerator, enamel stove, and heavy porcelain sink. On the wall near the door was a telephone. The one Cecilia and Ashley could not use.

Cecilia stared at the phone. It looked like an unattainable salvation.

"Sit down and let me give you the rules and regulations." Tessie cleared her throat while Cecilia and Ashley flopped into low chairs.

"First of all, I know all about you," Tessie began. "You've got a reputation from here to Kingdom Come as two terrible awful brats."

"Hey, wait a minute," Cecilia protested.

Tessie waved her hand for silence. "You've come to the right place. I'm a brat-fixer from way back, and you'd better know it. Whatever it is, it won't work with Aunt Tessie. Now here's the schedule." She paused, tasted something in the pot, added salt, tasted again, seemed satisfied, and appeared to have forgotten what she was saying. "Oh, yes." She remembered, pulled a chair up to the table, and sat down heavily. "Here's the schedule. You get up at seven-thirty, dress, wash, breakfast by eight-thirty, and work from nine to twelve." Her eyes glinted. "And I mean work. We're going to make this place into a paying guest house over the summer. You'll get your assignments every morning. At noon, when I ring a bell, you come in and wash and help set the table and eat lunch. After lunch you get an hour's free time. You can read or play Parcheesi or chess.

From one-thirty to three-thirty, more work, and from three-thirty till five-thirty, free time. Swimming recommended. At five-thirty you take a bath, dress, and help with dinner."

"What's after dinner?"

"Reading out loud and music."

"TV," Cecilia piped.

"There is none."

For some reason this fact struck Cecilia and Ashley as the very worst of all they had heard. It was as if the bottom had fallen out of their stomachs. "But I have to watch my shows," Ashley said pitiably. "I just have to watch my shows."

"No you don't," said Tessie. "It's no blood transfusion. You can get along without them."

"No we can't." Cecilia moaned. "We can't get along without our shows."

"Says you," replied Tessie. She looked at the kitchen clock. "Help, it's five-thirty, time to get the supper. Come on, now. I'll show you where everything is." She showed them where the plates and stainless were stored, where to find the napkins and the various platters and serving spoons and glasses. Dully, they set the table.

Ashley noticed that Tessie had handed him four plates. "Who's the fourth place for?" he asked.

"My wild Indian." Tessie grinned. "In case he decides to come out of the woods."

Cecilia and Ashley exchanged a glance that said, "She's the real article, a genuine crazy." When they finished with the table they sat down at it and watched Tessie don her apron and stir the contents of the pot again and finally bring it to the table. She lifted the casserole cover, and the fragrant, delicious aroma of stewed beef filled the room. Tessie spooned out small portions of stew and potatoes and filled their glasses with cold water. They ate gratefully. Craziness had not affected her cooking. There was no conversation and certainly no insults about the quality of the meal. They finished with a bowl of berries and cream.

"Are there any cookies?" Cecilia inquired.

"Not now," said Tessie.

Cecilia thanked goodness for the half-bag of M & M's she had stored in her dress pocket. They stood up and started for their rooms, desperate to talk and lay plans.

"Where do you think you're going?" Tessie barked.

"Upstairs," said Ashley.

"Not till you clear this table and wash and dry these dishes."

And so they cleared the table and washed and dried the dishes before they got to Ashley's room.

The door was scarcely closed when Cecilia whispered, "We've got to get out of here tonight, Ashley. I can't stay one night here. We'll run away. We've got to. She's a horrible wicked woman."

"Where will we go?" said Ashley.

"We'll just go the way we came. We'll walk down that dirt road, past the gas station and grocery store, and follow it to the other road and then follow that, and it will take us to the town and we'll tell somebody and ask to use the telephone and call Mommy and Daddy."

At the last three words Cecilia had such a keen sense of homesickness that she nearly fell apart. But her desire to get out of Aunt Tessie's house was so fierce that it gave her strength.

"Okay," Ashley said. "We'll leave after she's gone to bed. I'll give you a signal, three taps on the door."

"Do we pack our bags?" Cecilia asked.

"No, stupid. This is a getaway. We're lucky if we make it. We travel light."

"Okay." Cecilia was mortified not to have known this. Ashley seemed to have the upper hand.

"Now let's tell her good night. Tell her we're

34

tired and wait till we hear her turn in. Then lights out and listen for my signal."

"Okay."

They went into the living room, where they found Tessie in an armchair, feet up on a hassock, a book in front of her.

"Ah, there you are," she said happily. "I was waiting for you. We're going to read *Oliver Twist*. Draw up your chairs and choose to see who goes first. We each do a chapter."

Ashley and Cecilia did as they were told. After three chapters of *Oliver Twist* had been read, Tessie got out a set of Chinese Checkers and insisted on playing two games before she yawned and stretched and said it was time for . . . a cup of tea.

Would this never end? It was really dark outside. Tessie brewed the tea while Cecilia and Ashley fetched cups and saucers and cookies from a tin in the pantry. It seemed to take ages till the tea was drunk and the cookies eaten. Finally, the dishes were washed and dried and Aunt Tessie was saying good night at their doors.

Cecilia sat on the edge of her bed and turned off her light. She heard water in the bathroom. Sounds of teeth being brushed and of washing-up. She thought of the telephone. It had haunted her thoughts all evening, and now she decided to make a break for it. She tiptoed to her door and then down the corridor. She had her foot on the very top step when Tessie called. "No raids on the icebox or the phone in this house, Cecilia Melton. Go brush your teeth and wash up."

"Okay," Cecilia said shakily. She was certain that Tessie was a witch. Cecilia whizzed into the bathroom and turned on the faucets. She took water into her mouth and gargled noisily. Noisily she went back to her room, found the M & M's in her pocket, sat down on the bed again, and ate them one by one till they were gone. Through her window she saw a full, white shining moon come up. The ground turned pale. She saw stars and heard a racket of crickets. Moths bumped on her screen. There were three soft taps on the door.

"C'mon," Ashley said. "Let's go."

Chapter
5

To begin with, it was not easy to get out of the house. They kept bumping into things. The old floor squeaked loudly under their feet, sounding to their ears like explosions. They could hardly believe they had made it to the front door without Tessie's coming after them. Cecilia wanted to risk using the telephone, but Ashley shook his head violently. He closed the door behind them, and they breathed deeply. It was the first part of the escape. If they had done this much, the rest might be possible. By unspoken agreement Ashley was the leader, and he set off in the direction of the dirt road. The full moon bathed the clearing in pale light, but once they were on the narrow dirt road, overhanging trees plunged them into real darkness. Gradually their eyes grew accustomed to the degrees of darkness, and by holding hands and keeping their feet on a mound of grass in the center of the road, they stayed more or less on course. Fireflies blipped light around them, mosquitoes buzzed, frogs croaked. They walked and walked and walked. Cecilia's legs ached. This was not city-pavement walking. Pebbles threw her off balance. Dirt got into her shoes, and stones butted the soles of her feet. She fell down once and then twice, and the third time she knocked Ashley down too. They sat together on the ground in the darkness, knowing a terrible despair. Where were they? Who were they? Did anyone on earth exist or care or know? Was it all a dream?

As they sat, the muffled sound of a drumbeat joined the other night noises. Cecilia dug her fingers into Ashley's arm. "Ashley," she said, "what is it?"

Ashley could not answer. The drumbeat came again and then again. It was an ancient, slow, mounting, thumping drumbeat, hollow and clear and coming nearer.

"She said something about her wild Indian," Ashley remembered.

"It's a ghost. An Indian ghost," Cecilia immediately deduced, and then the strain and awfulness of the day welled up as if it were a fist and knocked her down. She lay on the mound of pebbles and weeds in the middle of the road, the picture of exhaustion.

The drumbeat all the while was growing closer and closer. They waited. Cecilia tightened her grasp on Ashley's hand, and they both stared before them at the dim outline of a man carrying a drum. Cecilia rubbed her tired dirt-caked eyes, and Ashley made a sound halfway between a hoot and a sigh.

The man knelt and looked at them closely. In the darkness they could only make out the silhouette of his body and drum.

"Running away from Tessie?" he asked. His voice was gentle.

In the dark Cecilia and Ashley nodded.

"She's a little hard to take sometimes, but a very good lady, believe me." The apparition went on in a whisper, "She means well." He stood up quickly and put out his hands. He took their hands, Cecilia's and Ashley's, and pulled them up. "Come home," he said. "Tessie will be worried sick when she sees you've gone."

They went with him gratefully. He led them, sure-footed, as if it had been broad daylight. There was no stumbling or pausing. Very soon they were back in the moonlit clearing before the old ruin of a house, which to their eyes now looked almost welcoming.

"Are you a wild Indian?" Cecilia whispered as they went up the creaking steps to their rooms.

"It's very late," he said. "We'll answer questions in the morning."

Chapter
6

Cecilia didn't awaken till the sunlight, flickering and bright, fell across her pale face. Ashley stood in her door. "Let's go down together," he said.

Cecilia blinked and rubbed her eyes and looked around the small neat room with her suitcase open in the middle of it. The most consoling sight in the room was her brother, Ashley, whom she had always boasted of hating. Ashley the weirdo, creep, doofus. Old horrible Ashley. At that moment Cecilia thought he was the best person she had ever seen. The events of their night slid into her waking thoughts. Her mouth drew down at each end. "What'll we do, Ashley?" She felt tears rising.

"We go down the way she told us we had to, and we have breakfast."

"What about the wild Indian?" Cecilia whimpered.

"We'll see." Ashley looked gray. "Come on, Cecilia. Get up."

"I don't wanna." She pulled the covers up over her face. She didn't want to let him see her go to pieces.

"We have to," Ashley said. His voice was flat and hard. It scared her and brought her head out from under the covers. "Get up."

She got up.

"I'll wait for you." He went out of her room and stood in the hall waiting till she pulled on her blue jeans and T-shirt. In the morning light the old house didn't look quite so awful. The cracking plaster and warped floorboards were not so much sinister as shabby.

There was a strong smell of coffee and bacon coming from the kitchen. Cecilia and Ashley remembered that they were hungry.

Tessie stood at the stove, her back to them. "Good morning," she said without turning around. "Go back upstairs and wash. That means teeth too, and don't come down again till you've done it."

They went back upstairs. Cecilia dragged her feet. "She's a witch, Ashley. She knew about us not washing and she didn't even look at us."

When they returned to the kitchen, bacon strips were spread on a paper towel and two mugs of cold milk had been poured. Tessie sat at the table. She looked at them. "That's better, much better. Now come sit down and tell me all about the Great Escape and how it didn't work." She laughed delightedly. "Or do we call it 'Wild Indian with drum finds runaways,' or 'Spoiled brats chicken out'?" Each time she produced a new title for their adventure, she grew a little merrier.

Ashley and Cecilia looked at their plates.

"What's wrong? You shy? Come on, you two. That's not your reputation. I thought you were gutsy little monsters. Bear tells me he found you about dead from fright, flat out on the road."

"Who's Bear?" In spite of herself, Cecilia had to ask.

"Thought you'd never get to it," Tessie said. She got up went to the door, opened it, and hollered something. When she turned back, grinning, the wiry dark apparition from the night before stood behind her. "Meet Ashley and Cecilia Melton," said Tessie. "Ashley and Cecilia, mèet my husband, Chief Masquag Flowers. I call him Bear." She nudged the Indian, and they both smiled.

Bear was such a pleasant-looking man that Ashley and Cecilia wondered how ever they could have been frightened of him, even in the dark. He wore denim pants and a white cotton shirt. When he smiled, he showed one gold tooth. He drew up a chair and poured some coffee into his mug. "They aren't bad kids, Tess," he said.

Cecilia and Ashley knew they had a friend.

"These two have a reputation miles long. They damn near did poor Cynthia in. I don't think she's over it yet. Don't be taken in, Bear. I know these two through and through."

"You just met them."

"That's right, I did. And they just met me, so right now it's a draw." She cackled.

"They'll work out fine," Bear said.

"They'll *work* fine," Tessie corrected him. "And I mean work. We have a lot to do."

Bear nodded at that, and said, "This morning we chip. It's a good day for it, nice and dry." Then, looking at Cecilia and Ashley, he said, "Tessie may

sound like a slave-driver, but she's right; we have a lot to do. We want this old place to pay off. It's our dream, you see. We've saved and saved for it. A house where we could take in paying guests and I could sell my crafts." Bear had a long dark face, and his eyes, which were like black olives, gazed at the old clock above the stove. "I'll tell you my dreams some other time. We'd better start work."

"After clean-up," Tessie reminded.

They took their plates and mugs to the sink.

"It's Cecilia's turn to do dishes," Tessie said. "Tomorrow it will be Ashley's, then Bear and then me. Can you keep that in your heads or should I post it on oaktag?"

"Why me first?" Cecilia said with a whine. "Why me first? Why not Ashley?"

Tessie glared her worst blue glare. "Because I said so."

Cecilia pulled herself up and stuck out her trembling chin. "So what if you said so. What if I say different?"

"You." Tessie lowered her head until it was level with Cecilia's, and her voice was low also. "You are a child, a spoiled and difficult child who does not know what is best for herself. You take your orders from me." She stood up again and without another word left the kitchen. Ashley and Bear followed her.

At the door, Bear turned back. "When you finish the dishes, Cecilia, come out to the veranda so that you can help chip."

Cecilia faced the sink and the few breakfast dishes in it. She could not have felt more like Cinderella if she had been told to clean out a stable. Her shoulders slumped and the usually truculent angle of her chin relaxed and her lips quivered uncontrollably. Self-pity welled up within her. She was no longer terrified, as she had been the day before. She was simply miserable. Misery of this sort was new for Cecilia. At home she gave full vent to her anger and terrorized those around her with the threat of her ill humor. In school no one was a match for her. The small school she attended was genteel and polite. None of the teachers had any idea what to do with Cecilia Melton. She could storm and rage and disrupt a class and then turn angelic and sweet, just as one of her teachers was about to weep. Tom and Julia were frequently called in, but no one could figure out what to do. Now Cecilia felt beaten and defeated as she washed the mugs and plates and set them in the drain rack. She dried her hands, sighed, and slowly walked through the house to the veranda.

Ashley was up on a ladder, running his wedge-shaped tool over the peeling shingles. Paint cascaded like snowflakes. Bear was doing the same thing on one of the columns.

"Hi, Cecilia," Bear greeted her with his gold-toothed smile. "Why don't you do the other column." He rummaged in his toolbox for a chipper and presented it to her. "You scrape away until you've got the old peeling stuff off as best you can. What you can't reach Ashley will get to on his ladder." She accepted the chipper and began awkwardly to work.

"Tap it where it's bubbled," Bear advised. "You don't have to work fast, but you do have to be thorough. I always tell that to Tessie when she goes at things like a house on fire." For a while they worked without speaking. The rhythmic scraping of the chippers and the faint clattering sound of paint mingled with the occasional bird and insect sounds of a pleasant warm June morning.

"One day these columns will be smooth and white," Bear said. "And up and down this veranda there will be rocking chairs, wicker ones, painted dark green. In each and every chair there will be a paying guest." He paused in his chipping to look up and down the veranda and smile, as if the guests were already there and rocking. "Tess and I have been thinking about this for such a long, long time."

"Did Tessie live in a teepee?" Ashley wanted to

know. She seemed to him much more of an Indian than Bear.

Bear laughed. "No, she lived in a little house in New Mexico not far from my reservation. She taught in the reservation school, and then she helped me set up my shop. That's how I met her."

"What shop?" Cecilia was getting interested.

"I make jewelry," Bear said. "Indian jewelry. Tess wanted to buy some from me. We struck up an acquaintance. She had an idea for a store to sell jewelry and crafts from the reservation. We ran our store for many years, and then she grew homesick for the East. We had an idea to take an old house and make it into an inn, where I could also sell my work."

Cecilia stopped, chipper in hand, and looked at the hopeless peeling broken veranda and the house behind her. She looked at Bear and experienced an unusual wave of sympathy for the gentle man. "But it's a wreck," she said. "Who would ever want to stay here?"

He smiled so that his gold tooth caught the sunlight. "Oh, it will be beautiful, you'll see. Beautiful."

Cecilia turned back to her chipping with a sinking heart. "Bear is crazy too," she thought. "Crazier than Tessie."

Chapter
7

They worked all morning. The day grew hot. Sweat made the paint chips stick to the back of their hands, cheeks, and necks. They itched. Mosquitoes buzzed, but the rhythm of chipping was hypnotic. Their thoughts traveled. From the look on his face, Bear was dreaming of an elegant, freshly painted veranda. Ashley's and Cecilia's expressions were harder to read. Cecilia's lower lip stuck out. She was killing old paint. It was war. Ashley was more peaceful. Only his stomach rumbled. Somewhere in the house a bell tinkled.

"Lunch time," Bear said. He put his chipper in the box. Ashley and Cecilia stood back from their work. The columns were now smooth, and half the window frames were chipped. They both liked looking at the job. The powdery heaps of old paint were like signs of accomplishment.

"Mine's smoother than yours," Cecilia said.

"It is not," said Ashley. "And I did more."

"Both good jobs," Bear said softly. Cecilia and Ashley were too pleased with themselves to continue the argument.

They followed Bear into the house, which was pleasantly cool. Without being told, they went upstairs to wash the paint off their hands. Something smelled very good. In the kitchen Tessie informed Ashley that he was to set the table. He did so, and then Bear and Tessie and Cecilia and Ashley sat down to a lunch of grilled cheese, tuna, and lemonade. They ate in silence until Bear cleared his throat and said, "The kids gave me no trouble, got the idea right away, and worked fine and steady. I think we'll finish the veranda this afternoon, including window trim."

Tessie nodded and gathered the dishes into a stack. "You get one hour of free time now. Your hour doesn't start till you've finished the dishes, Cecilia."

"Be back on the veranda in one hour's time," Bear said.

Bear and Tessie left the room. Cecilia placed the dishes in the sink, and Ashley sat on at the table.

"Mom's practically ready to go to Paris by now,"

Cecilia said over the running water. It was the first time she had thought of her mother that day. The thought of Julia flying off to Paris and Tom to California made her remember the plans she and Ashley had so confidently laid. Cecilia grew thoughtful and then sad. She looked at Ashley, hoping to find a mischievous light in his eye, but he too was downcast. Cecilia finished the last dish and wiped her hands. "Let's go out now and finish the stinking job," she said, "even if it is free time." Anything was better than moping around the house.

Bear was surprised to see them back on the job so soon, but he didn't say anything. At three-thirty Bear told them their work period was over and they could lay down their tools. "If you want to cool off," Bear said, "follow our road to where it forks and then go left. Walk three quarters of a mile and you'll see a pond on the right." He closed the toolbox and went into the house.

Cecilia and Ashley were amazed that that appeared to be that. No one told them to be careful or even asked if they could swim. They were simply free, as Tessie had told them they would be. They looked at each other and then at the road. "Come on, Ash. What are we waiting for?" Cecilia said. They got into their suits, took towels and fruit from a bowl in the kitchen. Ashley scooped up a handful of cher-

51

ries; Cecilia helped herself to a banana. With towels over their shoulders, munching on fruit, they set off down the road. As Cecilia neared the end of her banana she experienced a terrible craving for M & M's. A Mars Bar would do nicely, but the thought of an M & M made her weak with desire. She had never been seriously without M & M's and had never known what a wretched pit of emptiness could exist inside her. She would have done anything for just one shiny monogramed pellet of chocolate. She did not feel like Cecilia Melton. The heat was oppressive. There was not even a breeze on the narrow tree-lined path. It seemed the foliage was too dense to allow a breath of air through.

"There's the pond," Ashley said.

The path swerved sharply, and not too many paces from it was the bank of a medium-sized pond. A rickety wood-slatted dock, with every other board missing, stuck out into the clear greenish water.

Cecilia forgot about candy bars in her excitement. The wet soft grass was wonderful under her feet. In seconds Ashley was on the dock, preparing to jump in feet first. Cecilia watched him splash, disappear, and reappear, still holding his nose, his hair streaming.

"It's got a horrible bottom," he hollered. "Mush."

"Sissy." Cecilia lowered herself in slowly, hoping to grab the dock and swim off without touching bottom. But Ashley had stirred it up, and the soft slimy stuff was all around her legs. "Yuch." She heaved herself up and flopped on her back. It was okay after that. The sky, intense and blue, was framed all around by the tops of the trees that rimmed the pond. As they swam, they realized how cramped their muscles were from chipping and how luxurious it was to stretch and paddle.

"Is it cold?" A strange voice shocked Cecilia onto her stomach. Water dimmed her eyes, but then she saw a figure standing on the dock. A young girl dipped her toe into the water.

"No."

Ashley was on the far side of the pond, breast-stroking as if his life depended upon it. Cecilia, how-ever, watched the girl warily. She wore a bright orange bikini. Her straight reddish hair fell almost to her waist.

"Hi, there." The girl raised a long tan arm cir-cled with silver bangle bracelets. "Is it nice?"

"Yeah, out here it is," Cecilia called back.

"Okay, I'm coming." The girl dove neatly off the dock and swam a few strokes toward Cecilia, who remained in one spot, treading water and barely able to contain her curiosity. The girl stopped swimming immediately in front of Cecilia. "My name is Sage. Is this your pond?"

"I don't know," Cecilia said. "Maybe."

"If it is and I'm trespassing, don't turn me in." She had large blue eyes, pale lashes and brows, and patches of freckles on her cheeks and arms. Her teeth were large and even, but for some reason her smile formed to one side, which gave her face a tilted look. She had a clear bossy voice. "What's your name?" she demanded.

"Cecilia Melton."

"Nice," Sage said. "Did you make it up?"

"No." Cecilia had never thought of the possibility.

"I made mine up. I'm a spice. I thought of being Coriander or Marjoram, but who could waste time writing them." While she talked, she dog-paddled more or less in a circle around Cecilia. "So you don't know if all this is yours." Sage spread her arms to encompass the pond, and rolled her eyes mockingly.

Cecilia felt she was being taken for a dummy, so she had to explain. "My Aunt Tessie and Uncle Bear own the house. We just got here, and I don't know what else belongs to them."

"What house?" Sage asked.

"The ruin down the road." Cecilia thought she saw the crooked smile flicker.

"Oh, yeah." Cecilia strained her brain to think

54

up something outrageous and fresh to say so that Sage would know she was smart. "You know, the ruin with the creeps in it," she said. "My aunt is a frizzy-haired psycho with a limp, and Bear's an Indian."

"Uh-hunh," Sage didn't seem very interested. "I think I know who you mean. I don't believe they've been around long."

"No, they haven't. They're trying to convert the old place into a guest house. They'll work me and Ashley to death to do it."

"Who's Ashley?"

"My brother."

Ashley was swimming toward them with his face out of the water. "Who are you?" he demanded.

"I'm Sage."

Cecilia looked at Sage closely. She decided Sage was no more than thirteen or fourteen. "Where do you live?" she asked.

"When I'm not away at some school or other, with my folks, Mat and Emmy Packer. They own the boutique in town. I'm sure you've seen it."

Cecilia shook her head. "I haven't been to town yet. I don't think I'll ever get there. We don't get out."

"Too bad. Packers' Boutique is quite famous. Dresses, jewelry, handbags, and notions." Sage paddled off with these words, apparently bored by the conversation. She splashed and cried, "Race me."

Ashley made a great show of trying to catch her. They swam off noisily to the opposite side of the pond. Cecilia watched them go. She was very excited about this meeting with Sage. She seemed barely older than herself and Ash and yet so freewheeling and fresh.

After a while Ashley and Sage swam back toward the dock. Cecilia followed. Sage dried her long thin legs with a towel. When Sage saw Cecilia on the dock, she looked at her stonily. "So your aunt is going to make a guest house."

"Yup," Cecilia said. "And Bear's going to try to sell his jewelry."

"What kind of jewelry?"

"Indian. He makes it himself."

"Silver and turquoise," Sage said knowingly. "That's very expensive stuff. My folks had a few good pieces in the shop."

"Bear's is handmade," Cecilia said with authority. She had finally gotten Sage's interest, and she planned to keep it even if she had to invent things.

"Can you show me some?" asked Sage. "I love that kind of jewelry."

"Sure," said Cecilia. She wasn't going to back off now.

"Bring it down to the pond some time," Sage said. "If your uncle lets you."

"He'll let me," Cecilia said, silently hoping that he would even show it to her.

Sage put her towel over her shoulders. "Okay, see you around." She walked off slowly, a gangly figure. Cecilia watched her back till it disappeared behind the density of leaves. She couldn't wait till the next time she would see mysterious, glamorous Sage.

Ashley pulled himself onto the dock. "Who was that weirdo?"

"She's not weird," Cecilia protested. "I've got a date with her. I'm going to show her some of Bear's jewelry. Who knows, maybe I'll make a sale for the old geezer." She shook her narrow hips and crowed.

Whether it was an echo or an answering bird, they didn't know, but the sound was repeated eerily over the pond. Only it was the sound of reproof or warning, more like a moan. It seemed to say "Noooooo."

Cecilia heard it and her skin turned to goose bumps. "C'mon Ash, let's run back. I'm cold," she said.

Chapter
8

At dinner Cecilia said, "Hey, Bear, can I see your jewelry?"

Bear and Tessie exchanged a wary glance followed by a pause, during which Bear chewed a piece of bread and looked thoughtful. "Maybe later," he finally said. Then he turned to Tessie. "We should finish the chipping on the veranda by tomorrow. After that we can do the next job. The kids are very good workers."

Cecilia and Ashley almost didn't breathe after this compliment.

Tessie and Bear went on to discuss the work that needed to be done and how long each job would take. After chipping there would be puttying and then the replacing of rotted shingles, followed by painting. Then patching the roof and of course the installing of several new windows and fresh boards for the rotted and warped floorboards. Ashley and Cecilia began to tire of the conversation. They couldn't understand some of the words used: stripping, insulating, baseboards, plastering. Bear and Tessie made no effort to explain or to include them in the conversation. Cecilia and Ashley began to swing their legs under the table. Cecilia poked Ashley in the thigh with her fork. Ashley flicked the flat of his knife at Cecilia's arm. Cecilia howled.

Tessie stopped talking about gutters and drains and glared hideously. "Leave the table and go to your rooms," she said.

Cecilia had not finished her dinner. She had never in her life been sent away from the table. Quite the opposite had been her experience; she had been coaxed and cajoled, with bribes and pleading, into eating "real food." Any kind of behavior had been tolerated at the dinner table. She could not therefore believe that Tessie was serious. "I'm not finished eating," she said, forking a potato and ramming it into her mouth.

Tessie got to her feet. "Stop that now and leave the table, or you begin that walk back to New York."

Cecilia and Ashley stood up. "I hate you," Cecilia said, and rushed out of the kitchen.

When they got upstairs, they both went into Cecilia's room and sat down on her bed and looked for-lornly out at the branches of the tulip tree. Now Cecilia could feel the ache in the muscles of her arms and back and the exhaustion all through her body. She yawned. She was very tired. When she looked over at Ashley, she saw that he was fast asleep, sitting up on the bed. Cecilia walked over to the window and pressed her nose to the glass. She could smell the dinner. She was still hungry. Her throat closed off and she had to swallow hard. She thought up a letter she would write to her parents. She thought of the terrible things she had to tell them. For a while she consoled herself with these thoughts. Then she remembered Sage, and felt better still. In the soft evening light, she saw Bear emerge from the kitchen door, which was directly beneath her window. She watched him walk in his steady slow walk through the little herb garden and then into a thicket of wild fruit trees, so overgrown that in no time she could not see him at all. She felt wide awake and filled with excitement. What was he doing? Did he have a teepee out there as Tessie had implied? A hideaway, perhaps; a secret place? When he emerged from the thicket he was carrying something that looked like an old box. He carried it before him with effort. After the kitchen door slammed behind him, Tessie's voice rang up the stairs.

"Cecilia, come on down here to do the dishes."

Dishes? She had to do dishes when she had been refused dinner? Cecilia couldn't believe this new injustice. She would put all of it in her letter to her parents. Of course, from Paris her mother could do even less than her father, who was in California. But Cecilia didn't think about this as she stormed downstairs. She thought only of the guilt her parents would feel when they learned what she and Ashley were suffering. In the kitchen, her outrage increased. The food was gone, the plates stacked. Bear and Tessie sat at the table, eating strawberries.

"Your dishes' day is in effect whether you've been punished or not," Tessie said. Rage had replaced self-pity in the heart of Cecilia Melton. She was so furious that her tears dried on the spot. She went at the plates and pots much the way Ulrika had. Punishing them with Brillo for the wrongs done her.

Completely oblivious of Cecilia's anger, Bear and Tessie talked quietly about plans for the house and the craft shop. Between them on the table Cecilia noticed the closed metal box she had seen Bear bring in a short while before. Bear rested his hand on its lid. So engrossed in their conversation were Tessie and Bear that it was Cecilia who first heard the crunch of gravel under tires and the sound of a car's motor.

There was a tap at the kitchen door, followed by three more short knocks.

"Who could it be?" Tessie said. "We don't know anybody."

Cecilia turned off the tap. Her heart pounded.

Through the small fogged window in the kitchen door a woman's narrow face appeared.

Bear got up and opened the door.

The woman hesitated just outside the door. "Do you take paying guests?" she asked.

"We hope to," Tessie practically shouted. "You're about three months early. Come in."

The woman stepped in. One quick step and then she halted, blinking and nervous, under the light. "My name is Lily Rose Russell and the man at the garage told me that he thought you took paying guests and I certainly wouldn't have bothered you otherwise." She clutched a tattered canvas purse before her chest, and did not raise her eyes to anyone's face. Cecilia studied Lily Rose Russell. She was tall and skinny and what Julia would call "tacky." Old unfashionable clothes at least two sizes too big hung on her. "I mean, I'm sorry to have bothered you, and I know I should have called first. It is customary." She was stepping backward toward the door.

"Well, now, hold on a minute." Tessie stood up.

"We hadn't planned to take anybody till we fixed the
place up a bit, but plans were made to be broken. If
you don't mind the falling-down décor, we'd be happy
to have you at a very reduced rate."

The words "reduced rate" worked like pure
magic on the ears of Lily Rose Russell. They brought
her large eyes up for the first time and caused a smile
to form on her lips. "Oh, why that's fine, just fine."
She was practically singing. "I don't mind the décor
at all." She looked around the kitchen. "I love it."

"Go get your bags," Tessie said. "It'll take me a

few minutes to set up a room for you, air it, do the bed and stuff." She started for the door.

"There is one thing I have to tell you," Lily Rose Russell said gravely. "I play the viola and I practice. I'm up here for the summer Music Barn program. I'm in the orchestra. I hope you won't mind the practicing."

"Not a bit," Bear said. "Cecilia, help Miss Russell with her bags."

Cecilia ran out behind Lily Rose. An aged VW huddled just off the drive. The night was warm and full of promise. Cecilia wasn't tired anymore, especially when she thought of what Ashley was missing. Lily Rose opened the trunk of her car and took out one suitcase, an overstuffed briefcase, which she handed to Cecilia, a viola case, and a collapsed metal music stand.

"My name is Cecilia," Cecilia said.

"What a pretty name." In the half-dark she actually looked directly at Cecilia. Her eyes were light and veiled. "Do you enjoy music?"

"Sort of," Cecilia said. Oh, they would have fun with this Lily Rose. She followed the tall lanky figure into the house. Worms in the viola and peanut butter on the music stand occurred to her right off the bat. Ashley would have some inspirations. He was very good at this sort of thing.

Tessie stood in the kitchen, hugging a stack of clean linen to her chest. "Now, Miss Russell, come follow me. I'll show you to your room."

"Please call me Lily Rose," she said, flip-flopping after Tessie up the stairs. Bear took the large bag from her and they all four went down the corridor together and then waited while Tessie found the light cord in the room next to Cecilia's. It was a room identical to the others, except that the bed was stripped and there was a musty damp smell. Tessie opened the window with difficulty, letting in the sweet spring night. Lily Rose looked inside the wardrobe and opened the bureau. Tessie made up the bed.

"I just love it," Lily Rose said, confirming herself as an idiot in Cecilia's view. "It's absolutely perfect."

"The bathroom is to your right down the hall," said Tessie. "You'll have to share with Cecilia and her brother, but that should be okay. We're whipping the two of them into line this summer. Now, we haven't discussed rates."

Lily Rose twitched both eyebrows at once. "I can't afford very much."

Tessie laughed. "That's obvious. You wouldn't be here if you could. We won't ask very much either." She paused and calculated. "How's two dollars a day, till we get things in order. Food, of course, would be extra, but I don't know how much. I'll have to figure it out."

Lily Rose flushed with relief. "It all sounds truly perfect to me." She sighed.

"If you would care for a bit of fruit and coffee when you finish unpacking, you're welcome to join us," said Tessie. She had smoothed the thin blanket across the bed and plumped up the pillow and set out a towel and washcloth. "Sorry I can't offer you dinner; it's all eaten."

Cecilia thought, "Including what was mine and Ashley's. How could they have done it?" Her stomach felt perfectly hollow.

"I'd love a little fruit and coffee," the paying guest said.

"Then we'll be waiting for you in the living room. After dinner we read aloud and play games."

"Charming, charming."

Cecilia wanted to scream. She followed Tessie and Bear back down the corridor.

Tessie said over her shoulder. "You can join us too, Cecilia. Your sentence is up. Tell Ashley."

"He's asleep."

Tessie shrugged.

Just as self-pity had been replaced by rage, now rage was replaced by curiosity. Cecilia was very curious about Lily Rose Russell and the difference her being here would make. She thought of waking Ashley, but decided against it. This would be her story to tell.

Tessie put the coffee pot, cups, saucers, and fruit bowl on the tea cart and wheeled it into the living room. Bear turned on the lights. Tessie took *Oliver Twist* from the shelf. Bear poured out their coffee. There was a thumping on the staircase, and Cecilia was disappointed to see Ashley in the door.

"Come on in, Ash. Have a peach." Tessie beckoned. "You'll need a little nourishment before you do your reading."

Ashley grimaced. He took the peach and fell into one of the easy chairs.

"Rise up like a gentleman and say hello to Miss Lily Rose Russell, our first paying guest," said Tessie.

Ashley got up clumsily as Lily Rose entered the room and held out a hand to her.

"Oh, how very nice to meet you," she said. Then she looked around the room and her eyes widened. "Oh, I just love all your beautiful Indian things. The baskets and the pottery are wonderful."

For the first time Cecilia noticed the many odd-shaped decorated baskets and vases and bowls strewn around the room. They had looked like nothing at all to her. She couldn't understand what Lily Rose was fussing about. Cecilia watched Lily Rose carefully.

She watched her odd dainty way of sitting down. The way she selected a piece of fruit or balanced the saucer on the flat of her long palm, the little finger elegantly arched. Her voice sounded Southern to Cecilia, but she wasn't good at knowing that sort of thing.

"I would surely like to be included in your reading." She smiled. Her prominent teeth seemed to overtake the rest of her face.

"Just pull up your chair and clear your throat." Tessie passed the book to Lily Rose.

Lily Rose read in a smooth voice that rose and fell dramatically in the dramatic parts. She was an excellent reader, and before long Ashley and Cecilia were completely caught up in the story, wishing she would never stop. However, at the end of her chapter she looked up and blinked. "Who's next?"

"I'll take it," Tessie said. "You did that very well, Lily. Are you an actress too?"

"No, I've always been a fiddle player, but we read out loud at home. We never had a TV, so we had to think up ways to pass the evening."

Cecilia had never met anyone too poor to own a TV, and now she had met two of them. Tessie and Lily Rose.

Tessie read and then Ashley and Bear and Cecilia.

As they were going upstairs to bed, Cecilia tugged at Lily Rose's elbow. "Where is your home?" she asked.

"North Carolina. Why are you smiling, Cecilia? Have you been there?"

"Nope." Cecilia was smiling because she'd been right when she guessed Lily Rose came from the South, and she was pleased to have been such a good detective.

Up in her room, with teeth brushed, face washed, and lights out, Cecilia was drawn to her window by an odd rustling noise. She looked down through the flowering branches of the tulip tree. In

the moonlight she saw Bear, emerging from the kitchen door. In his arms was the chest he had carried earlier in the evening.

The squeak and shudder of a window being opened or closed broke the quiet. It was Lily Rose's window in the room next door. Bear paused, and, though he didn't look up, he stood very still for a moment before making his way into the dark shadow of the trees.

Cecilia wondered if Lily Rose Russell was watching too, and puzzling as Cecilia was about Bear's chest and where he was going with it.

Chapter
9

The next morning Cecilia awoke early. She was very eager to begin the day. She washed, dressed, and was down in the kitchen before anyone else. When she realized that Tessie and Bear were still upstairs, she decided to have a look around. She went out onto the veranda to admire the stripped columns, which actually shone in the morning sunlight, they were so smooth. She ran her fingers over the surfaces of wood and was proud of the way they looked. She wondered what the day's work assignment would be. Bear had said they would finish chipping today. With the thought of Bear, Cecilia decided to investigate the grove of wild fruit trees. She walked to the end of the veranda and then toward the herb garden just outside the kitchen door. She would follow Bear's route.

She paused for a moment under the tulip tree. She had an odd feeling that someone's eyes were upon her. She turned slowly, expecting to see Bear standing at her back, but Bear was nowhere to be seen. The only movement to catch her eye was at the second-floor bedroom window of Miss Lily Rose Russell, where a hand came to rest on the frame. Cecilia squinted at the window. This Lily Rose was quite a snoop.

Tessie opened the kitchen door. "Cecilia Melton, get into this kitchen and set the table. What do you mean, galavanting around when you've got a job to do."

Cecilia returned to the kitchen. Ashley was up. "This is not my dishes' day; it's Ashley's," Cecilia protested.

"It may be his dishes' day, but it's your set-the-table day. Remember to set five places this morning."

Through the window Cecilia could see Bear returning without his box. Ashley was thumping downstairs. "What does Bear go out to the orchard for?" asked Cecilia.

"To think," said Tessie. "Now do your job and don't ask nosy questions."

Cecilia set five places and put the butter, milk, juice, and cereal out on the table.

Before long, everyone was down. Tessie poured coffee and toasted some muffins. Lily Rose looked a bit puffy and unkempt in the morning light. Also, she looked younger than she had the night before. First she spilled coffee on her lap and then milk on the table. "I'm a little nervous," she said. "I go over to the Music Barn this morning. We start rehearsals. I always get these awful butterflies on the first day of any job."

"You'll be fine as soon as you get there," Tessie assured her. She poured a little more coffee into Lily Rose's cup.

"Well, they hired me, didn't they?" Lily said without much conviction. "They must have thought I'd work out."

"Have a muffin, Lily Rose."

Cecilia was surprised to see how thoughtful Tessie could be. She was as kind to Lily Rose as she had been horrible to Cecilia.

Lily Rose lifted a piece of muffin to her lips and Cecilia noted that her hand was trembling. Leaving most of her food uneaten, Lily Rose excused herself and went upstairs to collect her things. As she ran back out through the kitchen with her instrument case and sheets of music, she waved awkwardly. "See you all later. Pray for me, please." The door slammed, and soon the car started up.

"Poor thing." Tessie clucked. Then she reflected a moment. "No, she's not a poor thing. She's a lucky thing to be so interested in her work and to care so much about it. I hope one day you kids will know that kind of feeling, even if it makes you nervous." Tessie looked at the clock. "Speaking of work, Ashley and Cecilia, get going."

"It's Ashley's dishes' day," Cecilia said happily.

"And it's your beds' day," said Tessie.

"You just started that," Cecilia protested.

"Because neither of you made your bed yesterday," said Tessie. "Therefore it's got to be a regular job."

"That's not fair."

"Go up and make your bed and Ash's bed," Tessie said. There was a look in her eye that Cecilia knew meant "Do as I say or no lunch."

She had trouble making the beds. At home somebody else did it. She couldn't get the sheets to be smooth. If she eased out a lump or crease in one spot, it reappeared in another. The problem was maddening. Finally, after some time, she got her bed to look as if it had at least been straightened. Ashley's went a little better. As she worked, she thought of the chest and of Bear's hiding-place and of how at some moment during that day she would be sure to explore the secret places among the fruit trees.

When it was time to go down to the veranda and start chipping, Cecilia's head was so full of plans and schemes concerning the location of Bear's treasure that she couldn't wait to be started with her work.

The chipping went well and quickly. By lunch time the veranda was about done; all that remained was cleaning up and puttying the cracks. Lunch was uneventful and tasty. Tessie and Bear discussed the color to use for trim. They decided that the house should be white and the trim dark green. After lunch Ashley's job was dishes, but Cecilia had her free hour and this was what she had been looking forward to all day. When she saw Tessie and Bear drive off to buy groceries and gas, she decided that good fortune was with her. After sitting in the kitchen for a few minutes to enjoy the sight of Ashley trying to cope with the dishes, Cecilia yawned showily and announced that she was going out to try to find wild berries.

"See ya in a while," she said to Ashley, and walked slowly out the kitchen door through the herb garden and into the thicket of old fruit trees. She kept her head down and her eyes to the earth as if she were searching the ground for berries. Once in the heavy underbrush, Cecilia stood still to see if she could detect something that looked like a trail, some narrow path. She studied the ground carefully.

There was an area that seemed somewhat more open, where branches appeared to be bent back and where one could pass. She walked for a few minutes over what seemed to be trodden weeds. Sure enough, this rough path opened into a very small clearing in which stood a shed made of wooden boards with a shingled flat roof that had a window set into it. The ground around this shed or studio was flat; the weeds and vines and thorny branches had been clipped. Cecilia's heart pounded. It was Bear's hideaway. Inside the shed there was a bench, a work table, and shelves. On the table there was a box of tools, clamps, cutters, small saws, and files. Also, there was a stack of books and Bear's pipe. On the shelves were many boxes, including the one Bear had carried the night before. Cecilia never believed that her search would be this simple. As if she were dreaming it, she took the box down from its shelf. It was very heavy. She set it on the floor and then lifted the lid. What lay inside the chest increased Cecilia's sensation of living a dream. Bracelets, necklaces, and earrings of silver, turquoise, and coral filled the chest to its top rim. They were neatly heaped by size with bits of tissue between them. Some of the pieces had enormous, bright, carved stones and intricately worked silver. Others were simple, with stones cut smooth and flat in geo-

metric shapes and framed with flat silver. Cecilia picked up a ring and slipped it onto her finger. She ran a silver bangle bracelet inlaid with turquoise over her hand and looped a necklace of silver globes around her neck. Sage would be impressed, impressed to the limit. Quickly, Cecilia removed the ring, bangle, and necklace. The ring and bracelet fit comfortably in one front pocket of her jeans; the necklace was somewhat more bulky in her back pocket. She was sure it would look lumpy, so she switched the things around till she was satisfied. She closed the chest and put it back on the shelf.

All the while she worked at puttying that afternoon, Cecilia was certain that Bear would ask her what was in her pocket. But he was as engrossed as ever and worked without conversing. When the work period was over, Bear smiled and thanked them for doing so well. "You caught on to puttying as fast as you did to chipping," he said. "You've got a knack for it."

The day was muggy and oppressive. Cecilia and Ashley ran into the house for suits and towels. "Don't you want something to eat?" Ashley said. Cecilia was so eager to get to the pond, she had forgotten to stop off in the kitchen.

"Pick up a peach for me, Ash," she called over her shoulder. She couldn't carry any fruit because the jewelry was clutched in her hand and her hand was hidden in her towel. She ran as fast as she could down the dirt road. Ashley was too far behind to see her. When she got to the pond, she was disappointed to find that no one was there. She wrapped the jewelry up in her towel and put it under a tree near the dock and sat down so that she could face the path and by staring at it force Sage to appear. But the only person to appear, puffing and red-faced, was Ashley.

"Hey, what's the big hurry?"

Cecilia didn't answer. She was too chagrined.

Ashley kicked off his sandles and plunged clumsily into the water, sending out a great splash. Cecilia knelt with her back to the pond. She had counted on Sage's being there; she had counted on it all day. She was prepared with the jewelry. She was prepared to impress the living daylights out of that cool Sage Packer, or whoever she was. She sat for ten minutes, until she realized that waiting was futile and she was wasting her swimming time. She eased herself into the water, and without much pleasure paddled toward the center of the pond, trying not to stir up the mucky bottom. Cecilia decided that the summer was going to be about as boring as anything could be. She hated not having a single thing to look forward to except work and more work. She hadn't realized how much she had depended on the meeting with Sage; how the thought of meeting again had given excitement and drama to this altogether dreary place. She turned on her back and gazed up at the low humid sky. Boring and dull, that's what this summer was to be, and there didn't seem to be a thing she could do about it. Cecilia pulled up her knees and swam for a little while on her stomach. She wondered what they would have for dinner.

"I felt a raindrop," Ashley called out.

"So what." Cecilia looked up and her heart banged. Standing on the dock, in a long terry-cloth beach robe, was Sage.

"Hi!" Cecilia waved excitedly and swam in toward her. "I've been waiting and waiting for you."

"How so?" Sage scarcely looked up from the belt of her robe, which she was undoing.

"Because I brought some of Bear's jewelry for you to see. Remember I told you about it and you said . . ." Cecilia paused to catch her breath and to pull herself out of the water.

"So where is it?" Sage looked at her at last.

"Over here." Cecilia ran to her towel and quickly unwrapped the pieces of silver. Sage ambled up to her. She bent slightly to see the handful of jewelry. Together they inspected Bear's work. "It's nice," Sage finally said. She slipped the ring on one long finger and the bracelet up one long arm beside her own three bangles. She held the necklace up to admire it. "Really, it's okay stuff," was her verdict. "Thank you for showing it to me. Can I show it to my folks?"

"No." Cecilia was adamant. "I took it from Bear's secret place and he doesn't even know it's gone. I have to return it before he finds out."

"Okay." Quickly Sage peeled off the jewelry and dropped the pieces onto the towel. "And now for a dippy-dip." With her long legs she ran to the dock and, in the movement Cecilia so admired, curved her body and aimed it at the water. Ashley got out of her way. "It's really raining," he called to Cecilia. "We'd better go home. I think it may start lightning, too."

In many ways Ashley was scared of everything. His bravery was a phony act, Cecilia suspected. But she too had read that it wasn't a good idea to be swimming around in a pond in the middle of a thunderstorm. So she accused her brother of being a coward and then gratefully followed him back to the house. Sage swam around without paying any attention to the threatening sky.

As they went down the dirt road, heavy drops began to fall quickly. They were huge summer raindrops. Ashley and Cecilia started to run. The rain streamed over their hair and faces and down their backs. They threw back their heads to drink the rain. To be in a bathing suit in the middle of a warm summer shower was one of the best things that had happened to them since they had arrived at Tessie's. When they got to the house, Cecilia, seeing nobody around, decided to take the opportunity to return Bear's jewelry. "I'll be right back," she called after Ashley, and ran as fast as she could into the trees. The shed looked especially forlorn in the gray downpour, and Cecilia wished to be back in the house as quickly as possible. She lifted the lid of the chest and slipped the jewelry back in place. She dropped the lid quickly, certain that she heard something. There was a rustling sound, as if someone were pushing branches aside. Again she was certain that someone's eyes were on her. But when Cecilia looked out the shed, nobody was in sight. She ran back to the house.

"Hey, where have you been?" Tessie called as she raced upstairs.

"I took a short cut," Cecilia answered, but her voice was drowned out by the sound of Ashley's bath and Lily Rose's viola. "She was watching me," Cecilia thought. "She was looking at me through her window. She's a spy, that Lily Rose."

Chapter
10

"How was your first day?" Tessie asked Lily Rose when they assembled in the kitchen. Cecilia was setting the table. Lily Rose and Ashley had already drawn up their chairs. Bear hadn't come in yet. The rain had stopped, and a clear washed sky could be seen out the window. Even though they had been at Tessie's a short time, they had already caught on to the routines of her house. Cecilia was enjoying the table-setting. She had folded the napkins in a special way that she had seen in restaurants and had drawn a compliment from Lily Rose, who wanted to be taught how to do it.

"My first day," Lily Rose said, "was a confusion. Somebody brought the wrong music, and somebody lost the music, and somebody lost his cello. But it fi-

nally worked out. We're doing *Guys and Dolls* as the opening show, and of course the leading lady has a cold." Lily giggled. "In other words, it's the usual string of catastrophes. By opening night everything should be smoothed out." Lily studied the napkin she had been trying to fold in the shape of a cone and looked dreamy. "I'm lucky to have this job at all. My ambition is to play in one of the symphony orchestras, but that's a long way off, if ever, and till then I'll be happy to have a job."

Tessie was at the counter, molding chopped meat

into hamburgers. "If you stick with it," she said, "you'll probably get what you want."

"I've been sticking with it for a long time," said Lily Rose. "Music is my life."

Ordinarily Cecilia would have thought that anybody who said something like that was a doofus, but she was struck by the serious way Lily Rose had spoken.

"It is very good fortune to have a goal to work toward," Tessie said. "Bear and I have had a dream for years now, and we've saved up for it and planned for it and this . . . believe it or not, this wreck of a house is it." She winked at Cecilia. "It won't look this way for long, not with the kind of work Cecilia and Ashley are doing. This place is going to be a paradise."

These words of praise for the Meltons were the first Tessie had spoken. The impact of her praise was greater than any either Ashley or Cecilia had experienced. Cecilia turned to the wall, afraid the moment would pass too quickly or that she would do something foolish if anyone caught her eye. Ashley felt much the same way, because he looked intently at the tiled floor and flushed crimson.

"What's your goal in life, Cecilia?" Lily Rose said at last. "Do you have one?"

Cecilia hated to think there was something so

good that she didn't have. "Not yet," she admitted, "but I'm going to start thinking about it and not stop till I get one."

Lily Rose and Tessie laughed, Ashley joined them, and Cecilia was delighted to have said something so comical.

In the midst of this laughter, the door burst open and Bear, looking frantic and wild, tore into the room. "Tessie!" he cried. "It's gone!"

"What?" She seemed rooted to the floor. "What is?"

"The chest is gone. The jewelry chest."

Cecilia felt cold as ice. The kitchen was still, and Bear's despair engulfed them all.

"Oh, my God," Tessie said.

"Don't say 'I told you,'" Bear said.

"I wouldn't do that." Tessie shook her head sadly.

"But you did tell me, Tess. You always said, keep it someplace safe. And I always said, the shed is safer than the house; who'd ever look into it? Anyway, it's the place where I do my thinking and it's closer to the sky, and such places seem safer to me than any house." He sat down in one of the chairs and folded his arms on his chest. "Nobody but us even knew about my secret place," he said.

"That, as it turns out was not the case," Tessie

said very quietly. She too flopped on a chair. She looked at least ten years older than when they had been laughing just a few minutes before.

Cecilia was experiencing one violent emotion after another. Guilt came first. She had gone through Bear's things herself, secretly and like a thief. She hadn't taken his things to steal, but she had taken them for a little while. She also felt betrayed and angry. She studied Lily Rose Russell carefully, and deep inside she knew beyond any doubt that it was Lily's crime. Lily Rose, who had watched Bear carry the chest from her window. Lily Rose, who was too poor to have had a TV. Cecilia had never been so sure of anything as she was about Lily Rose Russell being the one who had stolen Bear's treasure.

"It's not only the money value of it," Bear was saying softly. "It's all the hours that went into my designs and my thoughts."

"The money." Tessie sighed. "It amounted to a small fortune in silver and semiprecious stones. Add to that the worth of your designs, Bear, and some thief made a very good haul for himself."

"I'm sorry, Bear," Ashley said.

Cecilia had never heard Ashley say he was sorry in quite that voice. He really looked so sorry, she thought he might cry.

"I'm sorry too," said Cecilia. They were all still for a moment, and then Cecilia slammed the table with her fist. "And I intend to find out who did it and get the stuff back," she shouted.

"Now that's the spirit," said Lily Rose. "Good for you Cecilia. Good for you."

"Trying to throw me off the scent," was the way Cecilia interpreted to herself this remark of Lily Rose's.

They ate, or tried to eat, in a sad and sorry gloom that night. Tessie burned the burgers so they were dry and crumbly. The potatoes, on the other hand, were crunchy and undercooked. After dinner Cecilia was so miserable that she volunteered to help Ashley with the dishes simply to share his company. Lily Rose went upstairs to practice. The mournful notes she played filled the house. After a while Lily Rose came back downstairs. Cecilia and Ashley played Chinese Checkers. Tessie had called the police, who came right after dinner and had gone out with Tessie and Bear to inspect the scene of the robbery. Poor Bear's secret hideaway was certainly open to the public now.

When the police left, Bear and Tessie went up to bed. Nobody had the heart to read that night.

Cecilia, Ashley, and Lily Rose followed them upstairs. At her door Cecilia turned to Ashley and said loud enough for, she hoped, all to hear, "I've made a vow, Ash. A solemn vow to catch the thief." She hoped Lily Rose knew what she was in for.

Chapter
11

All the next day they worked like demons, silently and
well. They tried to give Bear as little trouble as possible. They finished puttying and began to replace
porch floorboards and then shingles. The work was
engrossing and interesting. Bear was such a good
teacher that the time flew. Before they knew it, it
was noon. While Bear wiped his hands on a rag
soaked with turpentine, Cecilia watched his face. He
was so still, so quiet. His face was grim. The long
lines that linked the sides of his nose to the edges of
his mouth were deeper than before. Cecilia felt overwhelming sympathy for Bear. Sympathy was a very
new feeling for Cecilia to experience. She had never
felt it for a living creature with the exception of Cecilia
Melton. She was so fiercly sympathetic to Bear that

her usual intense emotions gathered with their usual ferocity and her eyes brimmed with tears. "Oh, Bear," she blurted, "please don't feel so sad. I'm going to do everything I can to make it right. I'm going to get the jewelry back."

Bear looked up, startled. He stared at Cecilia, and then his face slowly lost some of its sadness and he almost smiled. "Why thank you, Cecilia. I do believe you mean that."

"I do," said Cecilia solemnly. "I've made a vow."

"I appreciate the way you feel for me, Cecilia," Bear said. "Who knows, maybe your feelings for me are of more value than anything in the jewelry chest." He stood up and put his arm around Cecilia's shoulder.

Cecilia did not follow Bear's line of thinking, but she wrapped her arm around his back.

"Let's go in to lunch now," Bear said. He put his free arm over Ashley's shoulder.

That was how the three of them went in to lunch, linked together like old friends.

In the kitchen, Tessie said, "What's this? The Three Musketeers? Are these the atrocious Meltons? Am I seeing things?"

"They're good kids, Tessie," Bear said.

"Then they deserve some lunch." Tessie laughed. "Set the table and we'll eat."

The lunch was a delicious Greek salad with a loaf
of bread that Tessie had baked. "How's the work
going?" she asked.

Before Bear could answer, Ashley did. "We
started floorboards and shingles," he said excitedly.
"Bear is teaching us how to do shingles. Bear says
I'm good at it. Very good at it." Ashley was more
than just excited; he was radiant. He sat up straight in
his chair, his cheeks a high pink, his eyes bright.
Pride and pleasure created a light on his face. Cecilia
noticed it. She noticed how the sun happened to
come through the window at that moment and fall
upon them all at the table so that they were bathed in

its light, and she thought she would never forget the moment, for it was the best of her life. She loved everyone in the room, including herself.

"If you learn to do shingles, no matter what, you'll always have a trade," Tessie said with great seriousness. "All of your life."

This made Cecilia and Ashley feel grown-up and important. To think that they were learning something like a trade.

"Oh, this will be a very beautiful house," Cecilia said. "A very beautiful house."

"If only we don't run into any more bad luck," Tessie said.

"I'm taking care of that," Cecilia said. "I told Bear, it's my project, and I won't stop until I get to the bottom of it."

"Cecilia Melton" — Tessie waved her hand — "you are outrageous."

"I mean it." Cecilia said. "I even have a few very good ideas."

That afternoon Cecilia and Ashley worked so hard on the shingling that Bear's stolen silver was not on their minds. But walking down to the pond, Cecilia couldn't wait to tell Sage about the exciting events and her suspicions. She'd have her on tenterhooks.

"Why are you running ahead?" Ashley called after her.

Cecilia had seen Sage from a distance. She was sunning herself on the dock. Her long slender body glistened with suntan oil, her eyes were closed, and just to the side of her left ear a tiny radio sputtered country music.

Cecilia jumped onto the dock, causing the old boards to heave and Sage to sit up in alarm. "Oh, my God, you scared me. I was fast asleep." She blinked and slid her sunglasses up her nose. "Did you get the jewelry back all right to the hideaway place?"

"Yes, I did," Cecilia said breathlessly, "but you'll never guess what a horrible thing happened after that."

"Okay, so tell me."

Cecilia knelt beside Sage. "Well, we were all sitting around, me and Ash and Tessie and the paying guest, when Bear walked in looking like he was going to have a heart attack or a stroke, and he said, 'It's gone,' and Tessie said, 'What's gone?' and Bear said, 'It's gone, the jewelry chest,' and it was, too. We called the police, but it was just awful because that stuff was worth a fortune and it was just about all Tess and Bear had and we were all miserable."

"I thought you hated them." Sage yawned. "Why are you carrying on?"

This stopped Cecilia cold. She had completely forgotten how she had felt about Tessie and Bear only a short time before. She could hardly remember now what she might have told Sage.

"Maybe I did," she said shakily, "but now I'm their friend."

Sage removed her sunglasses and stared incredulously. "You're what?"

"I know it sounds funny."

"Funny? It's weird. Anyway, do you think they'll take you in to town now?"

"They never go to town," Cecilia said regretfully. "They get their groceries at the place just off the road near the gas station."

Sage seemed to lose interest and was about to lie down again.

"I have sworn to get the thief," Cecilia said in a low, gruff voice.

This brought Sage up again. "You have?"

"Yes, I have. I won't stop till I do."

"Any ideas?" Sage unscrewed the tube of suntan oil and commenced rubbing a glob of it over her shin.

"Yes."

Sage looked up.

Cecilia moved in close to her face. "That paying guest, Miss Lily Rose Russell, whose window overlooks the woods where Bear's shed is . . . Well I know for a fact she was spying at her window."

"You do?" Sage was as excited now as Cecilia. Cecilia was very proud of herself. "How do you know?"

"I've seen her in her window spying, that's how."

"Oh, boy," Sage whispered. "You're some detective, Cecilia Melton. Someday there's going to be a book about you, like Nancy Drew or Carolyn Keene or something. I mean it."

Cecilia couldn't tell if she did. She couldn't tell if Sage was serious or not, and this made her ill at ease. "I don't know about that," she said.

"Well, I do. I think you're amazing. You were amazing the way you found the treasure in the first place and then the way you observed this creep paying guest. Well, that's what detection is all about. I really do respect you. But what are you going to do?"

"What do you mean?" Cecilia watched Ashley lower himself carefully into the pond, thankful that he had no interest in this.

"I mean, you can't just accuse her yourself. Will you tell Tessie and Bear, or will you go to the police? What will you do about your suspicions."

"I don't know," Cecilia admitted. "I'll have to wait till the right time comes."

"I wouldn't wait too long, my friend," Sage said. "She'll have sold all the stuff and be on her way to the border by the time you open your mouth to say 'Wait a minute.'" Sage lay down on her back, winked and closed her eyes.

Cecilia guessed the conversation was over, so she joined Ashley in the pond. Her heart wasn't in swimming, though. She was preoccupied by what Sage had said. She had never really thought about what she would actually do about her suspicions, or what would be the best way to proceed. Probably she would tell Tessie. She thought Sage was right; it would have to be soon.

Chapter
12

"Don't bother to set a place for Lily Rose," Tessie said.

"Why not?" Cecilia stopped still with the heap of plates in her hands.

"She called to say rehearsals were going to run over and she'd get dinner near the Music Barn."

Cecilia returned one dish to the cupboard while her mind raced. Now was her chance. After she set the table she decided she would make some excuse to go upstairs and she'd get herself into Lily's room and have a look around. She would collect her evidence without having to worry about Lily herself turning up. She set the table quickly and asked permission to leave. Tessie was busy making a sauce. Ashley was on the veranda, admiring the new shingles. Cecilia went upstairs to Lily Rose's room.

The room looked much as it had the first night Lily Rose had moved into it, except that a pair of slippers was set by the side of the bed and a light gardenia perfume was in the air. Cecilia opened the top bureau drawer. It contained two scarves and one bandanna and a bundle of underwear. The next two drawers were even less interesting. They held a few sweaters and blouses and turtleneck jerseys. Cecilia opened the closet. She had to think of her mother's closets at this point, because the contrast was so incredible. Julia's closets (there were three) were crammed with clothes of every type and description. Evening, daytime, sport, opera, travel, spring, fall, summer, winter. This Lily Rose Russell had one dress, one skirt, one coat, and a wilted orange thing that Cecilia had seen her in when she went to brush her teeth in the morning. Cecilia was depressed by the sight of this closet. She started to close the door when her eye fell on two shoeboxes stacked in the corner. The top shoebox contained a pair of shoes, black low-heeled pumps, but the bottom box had no shoes in it at all. Instead there was a jewel bag made of embroidered Chinese silk and zippered on three sides. With unsteady fingers, Cecilia unzipped the bag. Inside, lying in silken compartments, were a string of pearls, a gold pin shaped like an owl with green stone eyes, a gold ring with a black cameo set in

it, and — Cecilia's heart pounded clear up to her eye-
balls — an Indian silver ring set with a large smooth
turquoise stone. Evidence. There it was; her evidence. She put everything back except for the ring,
which she put in her jeans pocket. She zipped up the
bag, stacked the boxes, closed the closet door, and
went downstairs for dinner.

"Cecilia, what's come over you?" Tessie said,
halfway through dinner. "You haven't opened your
mouth once except to eat. I never dreamed you could

be so quiet." Tessie studied her. "Are you homesick or just sick?"

Cecilia realized that she hadn't thought of home once all day. "No," she said. "Neither."

Tessie laughed. "I'm glad you told me. I'm writing a letter to your mother and I certainly wouldn't want to misinform her. I sent your folks a wire the day you came, just to assure them you'd arrived in one piece. But by now I'm certain they'd like more news. After dinner tonight we'll each write a message and I'll mail them off tomorrow."

Cecilia couldn't imagine what she would write to her parents. Something like "Dear folks, I am learning to do shingles. I haven't eaten an M & M for ages. I am different. I have a friend who's a TEEN-AGER and is named Sage and we tell each other things and I am about to solve a robbery for Bear and Tessie. I love Bear." Cecilia composed this letter in her mind, knowing that she would write "Dear Mom — I'm-fine-how-are-you-I-have-to-go-now."

"You can write your folks about how horrible Aunt Tessie is and how you hate her and how she makes you work like slaves and you think she's probably crazy and maybe dangerous." Tessie laughed and even Bear smiled.

"I won't say anything like that," Ashley said very seriously. "I'll tell her that it's okay here and I'm learning how to do shingles and have a trade for the rest of my life."

"Here's to you, Ashley." Tessie raised her glass of apple cider. "You two are working out better than I'd dreamed. Bear's right. Underneath your awful exterior you turn out to be two decent people. How on earth did my darling Julia allow you to get so awful without making you cut it out?"

"Mom's a softy," Cecilia said.

"Her being a softy made it hard for you," Tessie punned. "Now let's get on with dessert. I have concocted a truly brilliant fruit delight. You can describe it to your mother when you write." She got up and walked in her funny tilted way to the old refrigerator. Cecilia and Ashley cleared the dinner plates, scraped them, and set them in the sink. Tessie brought the bowl of fresh fruit to the table, Cecilia carried the dishes, and suddenly the door opened to Lily Rose.

"Why, I'm sorry to disturb you in the middle of your dinner," she began in her shy apologetic way which didn't fool Cecilia. She knew she had a bit of evidence that she would keep with her at all times, but she also knew that it was too soon to expose Lily Rose for the thief she was.

Chapter
13

As much as Cecilia wanted to concentrate on the burglary and how to solve it, her days were too full of work and activity for her to spend any time hunting down the thief. It seemed there was something to fill every minute. Chores for Bear and Tessie, combined with swims and long conversations with Sage. Time was passing very quickly. One day Cecilia and Ashley received a letter from Julia. "Darling Cecilia," Julia wrote, "please don't throw one of your famous fits when you hear this. I have bought you an irresistible jumper made of the thinnest wool in the world. It's lovely, a soft orange color, and I think you'll look divine in it (if we can keep the M & M's from hitting it too hard). And Ashley, love, don't zap your sister in a jealous temper, as I have bought you a really terrific silver jacket that all the French sports have made the rage." Cecilia felt this letter was meant for a pair of strangers. She no longer threw fits nor did she eat M & M's. Ashley hadn't zapped her once since they'd arrived at Tessie's. In fact, Cecilia would have to count Ashley as one of her best friends.

After she read the letter Cecilia grew thoughtful and downcast. However, her unhappy moments never lasted long now. There was too much to do and she was enjoying it all too much to be gloomy. Bear was in good spirits again, and work on the house was going very well. It really was beginning to shape up, and this was very exciting. Cecilia could see how guests would sit on the veranda or in the large pleasant living room with its beautiful Indian craft pieces.

One hot afternoon Tessie made an announcement. "Don't stay too long at the pond today," she said. "We're eating an early dinner. I've got four tickets for the show at that Music Barn where Lily Rose works. I didn't tell Lily we'd be there. Might make her nervous."

Cecilia and Ashley were very excited. This would be their first trip away from Moby Dick. Tessie and Bear had not even let them accompany them to the grocery. They had never been back to town. Cecilia told Sage as casually as she could about the evening's plans.

Sage was unimpressed. "Oh, yeah, the Music Barn. I haven't been over yet this year. It's a kind of a drippy summer-people thing." Then she thought of something. "Wait a minute. You'll be able to watch that Lily Rose. "You'll be able to observe her without her even knowing it."

"What do you mean?" Cecilia was beginning to catch some of the excitement.

"What do I mean? Isn't she the one? Isn't she the Prime Suspect? Or did you change your mind."

"No, I still think she did it," Cecilia said. "I'm waiting for more evidence.

"Then keep your eyes open tonight. Watch her; see who she talks to and how she behaves when she's not around you. You just might be surprised."

Cecilia couldn't get over Sage's savvy. Of course this evening would provide a wonderful opportunity to observe Lily Rose. She had thought only of seeing the show and had forgotten about the more important actions to observe. She mumbled her thanks to Sage for reminding her.

That evening, in a state of high expectancy, Cecilia took her bath and set the table, with this happy excited feeling inside her. After the dishes were done, Tessie told the children to go up and change into something nice. Cecilia pulled a pink-trimmed white cotton dress from her closet. It was one of Julia's favorites. "It's so simple it simply oozes elegance," Julia had said of it. Cecilia put it on hastily. As it fell over her shoulders, she found herself adjusting to it. It was light and thin and made her feel as if she could float over the floor. She had not been in a dress since arriving at Tessie's. Going down the stairs, she found herself moving differently, in a sort of glide.

"My, my, Cecilia," said Bear. "What a lovely young lady you are tonight."

A few minutes later Ashley surprised them. He appeared with slicked-back hair and his button-down shirt. But tidiness was nothing new for Ashley. Tessie and Bear were decked out too. Both of them wore silver and turquoise. Bear's bolo-tie was a huge rough stone set in silver and Tessie's squash-blossom necklace was both large and delicate in design. Cecilia wondered how she could have thought that Tessie looked like a crazy old lady. Tonight she was positively queenly. They climbed into the old car and were off. Down the dirt road in the summer night. Out on the blacktop, they drove straight into town. Cecilia craned her head to catch sight of Packers' Boutique. It was on the corner of Main Street and had a window crammed with "stuff." They passed all too quickly for Cecilia to examine anything, but she was left with the impression of a bright happy arrangement of dresses, scarves, and hats. They were out of the town very quickly. They drove for a while along something called Route 32; then they turned off this and began to follow signs marked MUSIC BARN. The Music Barn turned out to be, in fact, a barn. But it was an enormous one, painted red, with a parking lot, ushers to direct cars, and throngs of people dressed in gay summer colors lining up at a box office made of wooden slats. They could hear an orchestra inside, tuning up.

They were seated smack up in the first row. Almost directly in front of them, with her viola tucked under her chin, staring nearsightedly at the music before her, was Lily Rose. Cecilia was ecstatic. The lights blinked and then dimmed. The music began with a shocking volume. The curtain parted and the show began.

Cecilia and Ashley had been taken on a few occasions to shows in the city, but never had they enjoyed any as much as the one at the Music Barn that night. However, Cecilia did not allow herself to let the show carry her away completely. She tried to pay careful attention during intermission and to observe everything as soon as the lights went up. First she studied the members of the orchestra, Lily Rose included. Cecilia's heart nearly stopped. There around the waist of the drummer was a wide belt of silver disks set with mother-of-pearl in an Indian design. On the small finger of a tall cellist was a coral-and-silver ring. Cecilia waited for Bear and Tessie to notice, but they were too busy trying to attract Lily's attention, and then they were too busy laughing and waving when she turned around and saw them. Bold as brass, Lily didn't bat an eye. She just hugged Tessie and Bear hello and said what a wonderful surprise it was to see them all and stood there joking and talking. Cecilia couldn't believe it. Tessie and Bear simply didn't *notice* a single thing. Evidence all around them, and they didn't see it. Cecilia thought first of blurting out her observations to Bear and Tessie and Ashley, but then she changed her mind. This case was hers to solve. She would put it all together and when the right moment came she would point her finger. She had just been given a fine piece of evidence, but this was the wrong time to make an accusation.

When the show was over, they asked Lily to join them for a soda. With apologies and blushes, she told them the fellow on the drums had invited her out for a beer. Cecilia thought he probably wanted to discuss buying a bolo-tie to match his belt.

Before she fell asleep that night Cecilia decided that it had been the best day of her life. The work on the house, the swim, the show, the soda, and a whole new piece to fit into the jigsaw puzzle she was putting together that would eventually lead to the solution of the case of Bear's stolen jewelry.

Chapter
14

Cecilia had to decide whether or not to tell Ashley about her work on the case. She had often been just about to tell him and then for some reason stopped herself, afraid he'd make a joke of it and a fool of her. She had vowed not to tell Bear or Tessie anything. Her solution of the case was going to be her gift to them, and this gift would be spoiled if they had the least suspicion that she was at work on it. She now had more to go on than before. Lily's possession of an Indian ring (the ring Cecilia had never returned and that Lily had never reported as missing) as well as the several pieces of jewelry worn by her fellow musicans were enough for Cecilia, but she knew she didn't have enough for anyone else. She needed to trap Lily in an outright lie or an admission.

She kept guard over all her bits of evidence, hoping that Bear and Tessie wouldn't stumble on them. She would confide only in Sage. Cecilia wanted the case to be hers and hers alone. She puzzled over it in her spare time. But Cecilia did not have much spare time for puzzling. They had begun to paint the house with rollers and brushes. This turned out to be Cecilia's favorite job so far. She was a careful, neat painter. Bear praised her work. He said she was as good as a pro. Sloppy, messy Cecilia couldn't stand to spill a drop. She was doing the trim with a brush and had learned to measure the paint on it so that there was never too much or too little. Bear set up ladders. It was a big house. "Don't fall off that thing, for

heaven's sake," Tessie would holler. "We don't want Julia to sue."

Tom and Julia were becoming distant figures for Cecilia and Ashley. "I don't know if I remember what Mom looks like," Cecilia said one day when they were painting.

Ashley laughed. "Remember how we wanted to go with them?"

"Yeah," Cecilia said, her face suddenly sour. "I don't know why." Then she cursed because she had spilled a drop of paint. "I guess we've changed."

Somebody else who seemed to be changing was Lily Rose. She rarely came home after the show anymore. It seems that most nights she crept into the house long past the time when everybody was in bed. Cecilia watched through the crack in her door. Lily would carry her shoes and feel her way along, with her free hand on the wall. Cecilia could see very well in the dark.

"Harry and I went for a beer," she'd say through a yawn at breakfast, "and you know how things are. We got to talking."

Cecilia remembered that Harry was the drum player with the silver belt. She thought they had probably "got to talking" about a bolo-tie to match the belt.

"Then a couple of people stopped at our table and we went to this place to dance." Lily yawned again and took another gulp of black coffee. "Gosh, I'm tired." She looked tired too, but she looked better than she had. Even Tessie noticed. Lily looked happy, and that made her seem prettier. With her first paycheck she bought herself a dress. It was red and had a full skirt. Tessie and Bear said Lily looked beautiful in it.

Cecilia decided to keep a journal of the information she was gathering on the case so that no details would be forgotten. She was writing in her journal that afternoon at the pond when Sage appeared in a new bikini and matching robe. She also had a new watch, made of the thinnest gold disk.

"Oh, it's beautiful," Cecilia said. "Is it your birthday?"

"No." Sage smiled secretively. "My parents are repaying me for something. Something I helped them with." She oiled her arm slowly and then lay back and closed her eyes against the sun.

"Why are they grateful?" Cecilia persisted. She was bursting with curiosity.

"My secret." Sage scarcely moved her lips.

Cecilia jumped into the water. She wished that she could do something for Julia and Tom that would make them so grateful to her that they'd shower her with gifts. The only thing she and Ashley had been able to come up with that inspired gratitude in their parents was getting out of their sight. Cecilia swam around for a while and thought about this. Then she thought that if she could crack the burglary case, Tessie and Bear would be grateful to her. Undyingly, unbelievably grateful. Cecilia amused herself with daydreaming scenes of Tessie and Bear showing their gratitude. The scene where she came to them with all the facts, documented in her notebook. She would present them in a cool, unemotional manner, and then she would confront the culprit (Lily Rose) and demand the return of the goods. Oh, how Tessie and Bear would thank her and thank her and call Julia and Tom to tell them the news. Yes, she too would know what it was to be the object of gratitude. In the meantime, she would watch, observe, and take notes.

That night as soon as supper chores were done she hastened to her room, where she began to write down all her information. When she had finished, she read over what she had written, and she was disappointed. She didn't have enough. She was sure that Lily Rose had found Bear's treasure, stolen it, kept a piece or two for herself, and was now selling the rest to fellow members of the orchestra and cast.

Lily Rose's behavior further indicated guilt. She stayed away from the house more and more, got little sleep, and was now buying presents for herself with the extra money she must have gotten from selling stolen goods. Cecilia felt she was dealing with a sly, two-faced thief, and that Lily Rose could talk her way out of almost anything. She knew she needed far more evidence. Cecilia decided that she needed to focus on two things: she had to talk to the people she had seen wearing the jewelry and find out how they had come by it, and she needed to find out where Lily Rose had hidden the chest.

The very next day, after she had decided what she needed to know, Cecilia had a stroke of luck. It was just before dinner. Bear and Ashley were working over the outdoor fire, Tessie was fixing the salad, and Cecilia was turning pieces of chicken in a marinating sauce, when Lily Rose drove into the driveway. There in the car beside her, large as life, was the drummer, Harry. With her fork in hand, Cecilia joined Tessie at the door. Lily waved gaily, pulling the drummer after her as if he were a reluctant prize pet. He was tall and thin, and around his waist was the Indian belt. Cecilia could not believe her eyes.

"Hi!" Lily called. "Here's Harry."

Bear and Ashley shook hands with Harry, and Tessie inclined her head.

"I just wanted to show Harry this beautiful old house," Lily said. "I've told him so much about it and all of you."

"We've got enough chicken," Tessie said, "if you care to join us for dinner."

"I hope they don't like legs," Cecilia muttered.

Tessie shot her a look.

Any minute now, Cecilia thought, Bear has got to notice that belt. As if to direct Bear's attention to it, she fastened her eyes on the bright disks.

"That's a beautiful piece." Bear pointed to the belt. "It looks to be authentic Zuñi."

"Oh, it is." Harry smiled with pleasure. "I bought it in Tucson. It cost all the money I'd saved, doing a series of concerts out there."

"It's beautiful inlay work," Bear went on. "I think it was done by a friend of mine, Dwayne Tche-kai."

Harry took the belt off so that Bear could examine it. Lily Rose came into the kitchen to help out.

Cecilia silently gathered the cloth and table silver and dishes to take outside for the picnic table.

"Yes, it's Dwayne," Bear said. "See, he signed it."

Cecilia's theory was kaput. She had to start from scratch. No wonder Bear hadn't paid attention to Harry's belt that night at the Music Barn.

Chapter 15

Sage was very quiet when Cecilia told her that the theory hadn't panned out. Then she flicked her hair behind her ear. "Still, that doesn't mean she can't unload it someplace else," she said. "There are tons of other outlets. She's got a car; she could have taken the stuff over to Wilton or Essex or anyplace."

"Who could?" asked Ashley, flopping on the grass behind Cecilia.

"Lily Rose," Sage said before Cecilia could stop her.

At that point, she had to answer Ashley's questions, and before long she had told him about her theory and how it hadn't held water.

Ashley lay back and stared at the clouds. "The whole idea was ridiculous, Cecilia," he said. "All you have to do is look at Lily Rose to know she's too dumb to think of stealing anything. Anyway, she's busy being in love with Harry."

"In love with Harry?" Cecilia gasped. "I don't believe it."

"Tessie does. I heard her tell Bear that's what she thought. Lily Rose is always giggling, and now she keeps looking at her face in the new windows, plus she went and bought that dress."

"In a minute I shall be sick," said Sage. She got up and dove into the water.

But Cecilia was interested. It had not occurred to her that Lily Rose was in love. She had been so busy seeing Lily as a thief that as far as she was concerned Lily had no other characteristics. She was furious with herself for missing this. She was humiliated to think that Ashley had known something she hadn't.

"Boy, are you dumb," Ashley now said, taking advantage of the situation. "Pinning the whole theory on a belt and a ring. Everybody's wearing Indian jewelry now. Mom says it's the rage. She even designed a dress just to wear with Indian jewelry." He shook his head. "Anyway, I don't know if it was an inside job. I've thought about it a lot."

Cecilia realized that Ashley had theories of his own and that he was not about to share them. She was furious with herself. She stared gloomily into space as Sage hauled her long body up onto the dock and turned to face her.

"Hey, Cecilia, want to stop over my place for a soda?" She did not include Ashley in the invitation.

Cecilia was immediately transported out of her bad mood. She was enormously pleased. "Oh, I'd love to," she said, and then to Ashley, "I'll see you back at the house, Ash. Tell Tessie where I've gone. I'll be back in time anyway." She leaped to her feet, flung the towel over her shoulders, and marched off after Sage. As she followed Sage, Cecilia's spirits soared. She was very flattered by the invitation. It was difficult to keep Sage interested in a conversation. She was so easily bored. Sage didn't like anything very much. Cecilia found it a challenge to talk to her. The topics that Sage paid attention to were schemes for getting things out of people, mostly her parents. She wanted expensive things or money or privileges, such as throwing parties with no supervision or curfew. Cecilia recognized Sage's interest in these schemes because she remembered that she had tried out some of them successfully on Julia and Tom. But Sage was way ahead of Cecilia. Cecilia began to know something, however. She began to know that winning out over her parents didn't make Sage very happy, and that her success over Julia and Tom had not made her very happy.

The walk to Sage's house was surprisingly short. It lay in the opposite direction from Tessie and Bear's and was only ten or fifteen minutes from the pond. The dirt path turned, after a while, into a paved street, sparsely lined with lovely large houses and lawns. Onto one of these lawns Sage directed Cecilia.

A wide porch extended around two sides of the white-shingled house. Arrangements of lacy wicker chairs and tables added what Julia would have described as "charm." Inside, the house was airy and quiet and filled with the sort of furniture Cecilia thought was old and good. Sage looked neither left nor right. She walked in her bare feet over several Oriental rugs back to a large, light, modern kitchen.

"Sweetie, is that you?" a voice called out from someplace upstairs.

Sage opened the refrigerator and freezer, and banged milk, chocolate sauce, ice cream, and then two glasses onto the counter. "No, it's not sweetie; it's spicey," she yelled in a withering voice. She directed a foul look toward wherever the voice had come from. She dumped the milk, ice cream, and chocolate sauce into a cannister and set it to blend on a real, professional soda-making machine.

A tall pink-faced man came into the kitchen. "Oh, hi, hon." He waved. "My, my, my, who have we here?"

"We have my friend Coriander Cinnamon," Sage said without bothering to look at him.

"Another spice, is it? Two of them, I guess." He was a curious-looking man, both large and awkward. His pink face was framed with the gray hair of his long sideburns and goatee. "I'm Sage's father." He held his hand out to Cecilia. "Nice to meet you. Nice to see a friend of Sage's in broad daylight."

"We'd like a little privacy," Sage said, still not looking at him.

"I like my privacy too, Sage," he said, "and I think you ought to know that I have had umpteen phone calls today, both here and at the shop, all from the parents of kids who were at your party last night. They were throwing fits and kittens about how late that thing went on and the fact that Mom and I were out."

Sage turned off the soda-maker and poured the frothy liquid into glasses. "Just tell them it's got nothing to do with you," she said, as if she were talking to a child. "It's none of your business, what I do."

"There is nothing on this earth," said Mr. Packer, "that I would rather tell them than that. I am the last person in the world to try to interfere with what anybody does with her life. I'm simply telling you that I don't want a hassle from other parents."

"Okay, okay." Sage banged the cannister down with a loud clap and turned on him a look of such contempt that Cecilia was quite alarmed. "You get no hassle from me. I just like my privacy."

"This is my home, Sage," he said softly. "I just want you to remember that."

Sage did one of her sudden mood shifts. She shrugged and turned her back to him and looked blank as a wall. "Suit yourself. I don't care." She picked up the two full glasses and handed one to Cecilia. "C'mon, Coriander. Let's go to my room."

Cecilia followed her out of the kitchen. She cast a last look at Mr. Packer. He seemed to have crumpled near the refrigerator.

"Don't worry about him," said Sage. "He'll fix his first gin of the day, now that he feels he's really earned it. Actually, after what I just put him through, he'll think he deserves at least four of them before he and Mom leave for their party, and then of course the Official Drinking of the day begins."

Sure enough, the next sound Cecilia heard was the chink of ice against a glass.

Sage smiled wryly and closed the door of her room to further sounds. "He's an idiot, a poor sweet idiot. Actually, he thinks of himself as an advanced ten-year-old. He and my mother believe they are the charmingest children in the world. If you're lucky, you may one day hear them talk baby-talk to each other. But you won't because you and your aunt and uncle never go into town, do you?"

"No," Sage said sadly. "Aunt Tessie says we'd just be tempted to want things we don't need. She just goes to the grocery for food, and she sends away for her clothes through a catalogue."

"You're not missing anything," Sage said. "Believe me, that boutique is a bore. I don't know how they stay in business. They don't give a damn about it. They don't give a damn about me, either. He hates a hassle and she hates gossip. If I told them I'd sat stark naked for ten hours at ten below zero in their store window, my mother would say, "Did anyone see you?" and my father would moan, "Now I suppose the police will call." She sat cross-legged on her bed and sipped her soda. Cecilia sat on the floor. Sage's room was very beautiful. It was furnished with lovely antique pieces. It looked like the room of a young lady of the last century. There were bed curtains and ruffles and flounces and hassocks, and great bows tied up the curtains of pink-and-mint moiré silk. It was so lovely, but Cecilia had a sudden awful feeling that it was a room at the end of the world, cold and lonely and lost and filled with misery. She put down her

soda. She had to get back to Tessie's as fast as possible.

"I have to go," she said. "I'm sorry, I've got to run." She stood up. "Tessie makes us . . . I mean, it's my turn to set the table and get things ready for dinner."

"Poor old you." Sage drooped her lids.

"Yeah." Cecilia was at the door, waving her towel.

"I don't blame you for running out," Sage said. "I would if I could, and I do when I can." She didn't bother to show Cecilia to the door.

Chapter 16

Walking back to Tessie's house, Cecilia realized that it was the middle of August. Queen Anne's lace, chicory, and wild snapdragon grew by the roadside, and some of the wild apples were beginning to turn color. As she came into view of the house, Cecilia was astonished. She had not really looked at the place from a distance for some time. It had changed. The house was respectable and normal-looking. No one could call it a ruin anymore. The windows were clean and shining. The shingles sound. No rotting porch boards, no flapping roof. It was a pleasant house to see. Cecilia felt proud and joyful. Ashley was on the veranda. She waved to him. "Oh, Ash, it's so good to see you," she cried out.

"Are you nuts?" he said.

"Yup." Cecilia laughed.

That night Lily Rose came back from rehearsals with a new viola. The viola was new to Lily Rose, but had been made over a hundred years ago. "This thing cost me every penny I have," she told them. "But it's everything I have ever wanted." Cecilia's faith in her ability to observe was too low to analyze this new event. She didn't try to make much of the viola nor did she wonder where Lily might have gotten the money to buy it. She was unusually quiet at dinner.

"What's wrong with you tonight, Cecilia?" Tessie said over dessert. "What's got into you? Anything we ought to know?"

"Nope," Cecilia said. "Just thinking."

"I have something for Cecilia and Ashley to think about," Lily said. "It's something I hope they'll enjoy."

Ashley sat on the edge of his chair and asked to be told immediately.

"Next Monday we're starting rehearsals for the new show. It's *South Pacific*," said Lily. "I'd like to borrow Ashley and Cecilia, if they can be spared from their chores, so that they can see what it's like to put a musical show together."

Cecilia looked at her plate and thought that she would rather finish painting the side of the house. Ashley, however, was delighted. He loved the theater and anything that had to do with performing.

"I don't think I should stop in the middle of the side of the house," Cecilia said. "Though thanks for asking, Lily."

"I'll give you both the day off," Bear said, as if he were handing them a treat.

Cecilia couldn't bring herself to disappoint him, so she made herself smile and say, "Oh, thank you" and "terrific," and all the while she wished she could stay home and finish the side of the house.

On Monday Lily drove them over to the Music Barn in the back of her car. They sat among the scattered music sheets and old newspapers that Lily never seemed to organize or throw away. Cecilia had been too mortified by her blundering investigation to do much with it for the last week. She had made a few attempts to poke around in the weeds, looking for freshly turned earth, assuming Lily might have buried the jewelry. She hadn't come up with much. But she felt that her instincts were still correct, even if she hadn't much to support them. She wondered more and more about the viola. She had mentioned it to Sage, who said that old instruments like that cost a fortune. Cecilia had noted the viola in her journal, along with the dress and Harry and the possibility of

Lily's falling in love with Harry. When she had put all this down on paper, the thought came to her that Lily had stolen the chest and had given it to Harry, who was selling the jewelry for her. Obviously, he knew a great deal about it.

All these things were going through Cecilia's head as they zipped along in Lily Rose's car. At the Music Barn, Lily told Ashley and Cecilia where to sit. The theater looked huge and empty. Then she left them for her own chair in the orchestra. The cast began to drift in, and so did the musicians. They wore shorts and slacks and sandals. They wore something else. Ashley was the first to notice it.

"Hey, Cissy, look," he whispered in her ear.

"At what?"

"Everybody's wearing Indian jewelry."

Cecilia thought he was teasing her. She yawned. "Yeah, so what. It's a fad. You told me."

"But not like that." Ashley wasn't kidding.

Cecilia leaned forward and narrowed her eyes. It really was incredible. The men had thick rings and bolo-ties and belts. The women wore bangle bracelets, necklaces, and rings.

"This is an epidemic," Ashley said.

In fact, before the conductor came on and tapped his stick for attention, the members of the cast were standing about on stage, admiring each other's jewelry and holding up pieces of it to examine.

"Listen." Ashley was getting very excited. "Cecilia, something is up this time. Something is very fishy."

The conductor tapped again for silence and raised his baton (his watchband was silver and turquoise). The music started. Cecilia and Ashley could hardly pay attention. They were about to jump out of their skins. The Indian jewelry display on the stage of the Music Barn was colossal.

"You may have been wrong last time," Ashley said. "But this is something different."

"Why did Lily bring us over to see this?" Cecilia said in a whisper.

"Because she set it up last time with Harry's belt."

"You mean, you think she purposely brought him over in his belt so that none of us would be suspicious later on?" Cecilia sank lower in her chair. "It doesn't make any sense. Something is wrong with it." She couldn't hear anything on stage, and she couldn't see anything but the jewelry, and she kept thinking and thinking of what it all could mean.

At the lunch break, Lily joined them and asked if they wished to be introduced to any of the cast before she drove them home. Ashley wanted to meet the two stars of the show. Lily took them both up on stage and introduced them to Sally Courten, the leading lady. On her wrist there was the same bangle bracelet Cecilia remembered taking from Bear's chest to show Sage.

"How do you do?" Cecilia said in her best voice,

and then she took the plunge. "That's a beautiful bracelet."

"Thank you, darling," Miss Courten gushed. "I adore it. We all went into town yesterday and found this divine little place where they have fantastic Indian jewelry for incredibly reasonable prices. Harry, our drummer, knows all about this stuff, and he says it's worth twice what we paid. We very nearly bought out the entire collection."

Cecilia darted a look at Lily Rose, who turned pale and tense. "Is that right?" she said.

Cecilia couldn't sort all this out. Lily Rose must have given the jewelry to Harry, and he was selling it from some little place. Lily Rose seemed very eager to get the Meltons out of the theater now. She was hurrying them down the steps of the stage and out the door. Though they had been introduced only to one "star," and people called or waved to Lily, she didn't even respond. She was very intent on leaving. Driving back to the house, Lily was so preoccupied that she scarcely made any conversation. She asked how they liked the rehearsal, but did not listen to their answers. Something was cooking.

Tessie had a fruit salad set on the table for them when they arrived. "I know you have only an hour for lunch, Lily," she said, "so let's sit right down."

"Tessie, I've got to leave now," Lily replied in a

very serious voice. "Something has come to my attention regarding Bear's jewelry, and I've got to check it out. I don't want to talk about it yet, but if my theory is correct I think we're close to finding out what happened to it."

Cecilia was panicky. She knew that Lily knew that she and Ashley were on to her, so she was planning a quick getaway. Cecilia felt that she had to stop Lily. It was now or never. She didn't have time to consult her journal. She cleared her dry throat, and then sat down because her legs felt weak. "Wait a minute, Lily," she said. "I suppose we all have a theory. Can I tell mine?" Without waiting for an answer, she began. "My theory," she said slowly, "is that the thief was somebody really poor who just happened to see Bear from her window or maybe going into the woods and wondered where he was going and got curious and decided to follow him and then found his hideaway and the chest and opened it and got all excited about it and thought, WOW, here I am poor and hard-working and look what I found and now I'll be rich and lazy and take it back to my room and hide it and then put it in my car and sell it piece by piece to all the new people I've met at work and be able to afford dresses and things I always wanted." As she spoke, Cecilia watched Lily Rose carefully. She knew that detectives observed suspects minutely when expounding their theories and could learn a great deal from sudden blushes, twitches, or nervous ticks. Of course, what she really hoped for was a shriek of "I did it, I did it," or "Are you accusing me?" Cecilia was watching Lily Rose so carefully that she did not notice Tessie watching *her*. In fact, she didn't take her eyes off Lily Rose until she heard Tessie's low flat voice say, "Cecilia, what window? What room?"

Cecilia was shocked. "Oh, why any window, Tessie."

"But *any* window does not face out on Bear's woods."

"Mine does, and so does Lily Rose's," said Cecilia.

Tessie went on ominously. "Cecilia Melton, tell me the truth. Are you describing the way *you* found Bear's hideaway? No one will be angry with you. Just tell us the truth."

Cecilia couldn't believe it. Tessie thought she was talking about herself, not Lily Rose. She had completely missed the point. She was angry and hurt. "Tell the truth?" she cried. "Tell the TRUTH?"

"Yes, if there is anything you feel you have to tell us, just say it out."

Cecilia jumped off her seat and upset the chair. She had certainly staged many phony fits in her life, but now she was going to have a real one. "It wasn't me who spied from my window; it was her. Lily Rose. I saw her myself. I saw her watching Bear. I heard her."

"Stop this instant," Tessie said. "You are inventing this."

"I am not," Cecilia hollered. "I have evidence."

"Evidence?" Tessie was pale.

"I examined her room weeks ago, and look what I found in her jewel case." Cecilia pulled the ring from her pocket and held it up, on the palm of her hand. "One of Bear's rings."

"One of Bear's rings?" Now it was Lily Rose's turn to stand up and overturn her chair. "That's my ring. I've had it for years. I thought I'd lost it at work."

"The jewelry I saw at the Music Barn today, Miss Courten's bracelet, I know that was Bear's. I saw it in his chest," Cecilia said before she knew it.

Tessie said, "Cecilia, how do you know what Bear's jewelry looks like? When did you see his chest?"

They all looked at Cecilia. She stood very still, letting their eyes take her in. She knew what they thought. She knew they had made up their minds. She felt wronged and trapped. "Because I found the chest too," she said. "But I didn't touch a thing." She paused and saw Tessie nod as if she'd known it all along, and Cecilia said. "I hate you, I hate you," and threw the silver ring at her. "You treat us like slaves and then accuse us of things."

"Cecilia," Tessie said sternly "you are the one who did the accusing. I think you owe Miss Russell an apology. You owe us all an apology for this display of temper."

"She stole Bear's jewelry and sold it and bought a viola and a dress and I won't apologize to her or anybody," Cecilia yelled. Then she ran out of the kitchen and up the stairs to her own room.

She threw herself down on the bed, intending to howl and scream, but no sounds came. She lay rigid.

She had been the best Cecilia she had ever been in her life. She had even decided to love them, and what had it gotten her? It had gotten her their distrust and disapproval. She was better off when she behaved horribly; at least she could not be hurt. She knew where she stood. She was atrocious Cecilia. Now who was she? She would have to leave. She knew that Ashley wouldn't come and that she was on her own.

Chapter
17

She couldn't believe how easy it was. She simply left. She got up off her bed, folded into her sneaker the dollar bill Julia had given her, walked down the stairs, passed the kitchen, where she could hear their voices, and into the drive, where Lily's car was parked. Cecilia walked past the car without turning her head once. She walked down the dirt road, turned right onto the blacktop, and kept going. It was so simple. She passed the gas station, the small bunches of houses, and in less than thirty minutes she was in the town of Upton Manor.

She knew exactly what to do. She went into the drug store phone booth and dialed Julia's New York office.

"A collect call for Mrs. Melton from Cecilia Melton," she said in her strongest voice.

"I'll take the charges," Julia's secretary, Min Wheeler, boomed. "Cissy, how are you?"

Cecilia said, "Where's my mother?"

"She's with your Dad on the Coast, honey. Everything okay?"

"Call her right away and tell her to come for me. Tell her not to call Tessie's, but to come, because some terrible things have happened."

"Cecilia . . ." Min's voice dropped several octaves. "Honey, can we talk about this. Like, where are you calling from and is your Aunt Tessie around?"

"I can't tell you anything more than what I just said." Cecilia realized that Min was stalling for time, and she didn't like it, so she did something she hadn't done for weeks. She forced herself to throw a fake fit.

She shrieked and screamed and, though it all sounded rusty and false to her ears, it worked.

"Oh, God," Min cried. "Cissy, please stop. I'll call your mom this minute. Right away. Oh, stop."

Cecilia hung up.

Now she had to think of what to do next. She knew she would have to go back to Tessie's, but she wasn't eager to do so. She lingered in the drug store for a while and looked at the displays. She bought herself a large package of M & M's and ate them several at a time. Their sweetness was at first a shock to her mouth. She left the drug store and ambled down the street. Then she stopped dead in her tracks. Lily Rose's car was parked in front of Packers' Boutique. Lily Rose was getting out of her car. She saw Cecilia, and Cecilia saw her. Lily Rose held out her hand.

"Come with me, Cecilia. Let's get to the bottom of this thing," she said. "You told me your theory, now let's check into mine. Packers is the place where the cast got all that jewelry, I didn't want to tell Bear and Tessie and raise their hopes, but this is worth looking into. Since you can identify some of the pieces, you can judge better than I if any of this is Bear's. If you see a piece in the shop that you can definitely identify as Bear's, give me a sign, Cecilia. Pinch my arm very very hard."

As they entered the shop, a bell chimed, and the scent of jasmine incense greeted them.

"Can I help you?" a woman in a pink dress leaned over a counter.

"Not just yet," Lily Rose drawled. "We'd like to look around. You have so many pretty things."

"Take your time. Let me know if I can be of help." The woman smiled. Her pink-lipsticked mouth was the same color as the dress, and in shape almost identical to Sage's. Her eyes, too, were the same color as Sage's, and under her powder there were faint freckles. The shop resembled a wonderful living room. There were Victorian rockers and little needlepoint-covered benches, on which blouses and handbags and belts were casually placed. Slowly, Lily Rose made her way around the room with Cecilia at her side. Periodically she would exclaim enthusiastically to Cecilia over some item or another. "Just look at that cunning little evening purse, honey. Wouldn't that do fine for Auntie's birthday?"

"Auntie's birthday?"

"You know," Lily Rose said. "Auntie's gift, honey. That's what we're here looking for. Pay attention. Now let's see, maybe she'd rather have a chiffon scarf. She's got such fine taste it kind of scares me to buy anything for her." This, Lily Rose said over her shoulder, more to the saleslady than to Cecilia. "She's so sophisticated and what-all. Now let's see." They approached a glass cabinet, within which lay a collection of Indian jewelry.

"Let's see." Lily Rose and Cecilia studied the objects in the cabinet. "Oh, my, what lovely jewelry. OUCH." Lily winced and rubbed her arm. Cecilia smiled to herself.

"Yes, indeed," the saleswoman said. "If your aunt is a woman of taste, she'll not find fault with these pieces. They're really beautiful. You're lucky to see them here at all. I had a whole bunch of peo-

ple from the Music Barn in yesterday and they nearly cleaned out the entire collection."

"You don't say."

"It was the very first day I put them out, too. I think by tomorrow there won't be a piece left."

"Mmmmm-hmmm." Lily Rose squinted at the jewelry. "They are sweet. I don't know anything about this kind of work. Is it Zuñi or Pueblo or something?"

"It's authentic." The saleslady looked a bit puzzled herself. "But to tell you the truth, I don't know what tribe it's from."

"Well, honey" — Lily was becoming more Southern by the minute — "where did you find it?"

The saleswoman with Sage's mouth smiled. "I got it in the darnedest way," she said. "My daughter bought the entire collection from an old woman she met swimming one afternoon. She came home with this chest filled to the top with jewelry. She told me she'd spent her entire allowance plus her savings on the jewelry. At first I thought I'd be fit to be tied, that someone had ripped her off, but when I looked at it I had to congratulate her."

"My, my," Lily Rose said admiringly, "what a clever child."

"Yes, she is. We've had no end of trouble with

143

her. No school will keep her. She breaks every rule and all that, but I said to my husband, we don't have to worry about our Lucile. She's got a fine business sense that we never even knew about. She asked us to sell the stuff for her and I told her she can save up her profits for another venture if she likes."

"Isn't that wonderful."

"You never know with these kids." Mrs. Packer marveled. "You think they're nothing but a pain in the neck and then all of a sudden they do something that just makes you stop and wonder." She smiled her super pink-and-white smile again.

In a voice so low she could hardly be heard, Cecilia said, "Does Lucile some times call herself Sage?"

"Yes, indeed, she does." Mrs. Packer giggled. "She's Sage. Can you imagine? Have you met her?"

"Uh-hunh."

"Honey, I just love this jewelry," said Lily, almost crooning. "But I'd better think it over for a minute before I make the big decision. My little sister and I will get us a soda and think what to do. Come along, little sister. We'll be back in a flash, now." Lily Rose pulled Cecilia toward the door.

"Now we call Bear and Tessie," said Lily Rose in her regular voice, "and we make it snappy. I have to be back at work by one-thirty. Incidentally, you have very strong fingers, Cecilia. You could play the fiddle." Lily rubbed her arm.

After that everything happened at once. Tessie and Bear were called and came. The minute they entered the shop, Mrs. Packer seemed to sense that something unpleasant was about to happen. Bear carried his album of photographs of each piece of jewelry he had made. Cecilia explained that she had been the one to tell Sage about the jewelry. Then she confessed that she had found the shed where Bear worked and had taken a few pieces to show Sage. She guessed that Sage had followed her from the pond that day, back to the shed, and had simply taken the chest after Cecilia left.

Mrs. Packer called her husband from the back of the shop. "Hi," he said when he recognized Cecilia. "Where have you been?" Then he, too, realized that the people in the shop were not casual shoppers. He saw the open album of photos, and Mrs. Packer told him the story. "She's stolen a few things before," Mr. Packer said. "Nothing much — some money from my wallet, a few things from friends' houses. I never mentioned it of course; it didn't seem that important. Kids do that sort of thing, and I didn't want a hassle. I mean, she never stole like this."

Mrs. Packer's face had become very pale and her hands were trembling. "Look, please, don't *do* anything about this. I mean, don't call the police or anything. We can settle this between ourselves. Sage is so young. We'll do whatever you wish. If you like, we can recall the pieces we sold and return the money to the buyers or we can turn over to you all the money we received. We'll take no commission for ourselves. Only please leave Sage out of it."

"We've had such a time with her," Mr. Packer said. He took a small box of pills out of a drawer and, after taking one, passed the box to his wife. They swallowed their pills without water.

"She must be going through something, some phase," Mrs. Packer said.

"It's none of my business," Tessie remarked icily. "But it seems to me she'll go through this phase into a worse one unless you do something fast. Your little girl is headed for big trouble."

"What can we do?" Mr. Packer wailed. "We've given her everything. She doesn't have to steal."

"Give her a job," Tessie snapped. "Put the brat to work. She has no business hanging around ponds and making trouble all summer. Put her to work in this store."

Mrs. Packer looked horrified. "Oh, but she'd get bored."

"And in your hair," Tessie finished. "That's what you mean."

Bear said he'd think about taking the money when he had gone over the receipts of the jewelry sales.

So many things had happened that day. So many mysteries had been solved. Cecilia had to form a whole new set of opinions. New opinions about Lily Rose and new opinions about Sage. She thought she also had a new opinion of herself. She felt she was a different Cecilia, removed by miles and years from the Cecilia who had arrived at Upton Manor in June. She liked the new Cecilia; she wanted more than anything to hold on to her and not leave her behind at Upton Manor in the fall. She wanted to take her back to New York, to Tom and Julia. She was afraid that this would not be easy.

Chapter
18

"Lily Rose," said Cecilia the next morning at breakfast. "I have to apologize to you, and if I were you I wouldn't accept the apology."

"Why ever not?" asked Lily, looking up from a music score.

"Because I was horrible to you all summer. I thought you were the thief."

"It worked out anyway," said Lily, who seemed embarrassed. "I do accept your apology, Cecilia. Now buzz off; I've got to study this score or I'm dead."

Cecilia finished her breakfast and chores and then went outside to paint the house. Ashley was already stirring the creamy liquid in the buckets and wiping the turpentine off his brush. Cecilia stood admiring her work for a few minutes. Then she took her bucket from Ashley and climbed the ladder to the spot where she had left off two days before. With small expert movements she dipped her brush and started to paint. It had become Cecilia's habit, while she was painting, to let her thoughts range over many subjects, free-floating, touching on this and that. Today, she thought of Sage–Lucile and how she had been deceived by her. Tessie had said that Sage was headed for big trouble. Cecilia knew how easy it was to get started doing something you really hated and didn't like yourself for doing, but just couldn't stop. She had never much liked the way she was, but she didn't know what else she could be. Cecilia thought how lucky she and Ashley were to have landed themselves at Tessie's, where they'd been given a chance to stop being what they didn't like and start finding out what they did. She was so absorbed by all these thoughts that it wasn't until the car had pulled right up to the door, and the cries of "Halloo darlings" were filling the air, that Cecilia saw Julia and Tom emerging from their dusty purple Porsche.

Tessie came out of the house; Ashley came down from his ladder; Bear came in from the woods. Only Cecilia stood stock-still, up on her ladder. The telephone call. She had completely forgotten.

Julia looked awful. To no one in particular she

said, "What happened?" and then to Tessie, "What have they done now?" She clutched her purse to her side. "There was this terrible, alarming telephone call. We took the very first plane we could."

"It's obvious the kids are just fine," said Tom.

Then Julia focused for the first time on Ashley and Cecilia, and her face relaxed somewhat. "Yes, oh yes!" she cried, and she hugged Ashley and then Tessie and then Cecilia, who had come down from the ladder. "Darling child, what are you doing with that brush? Aunt Tessie can't approve of such a project. Good Lord, what would the painters say?"

"We're the painters," Ashley said.

"Yes, of course, dear," Julia said, humoring him. She had regained her usual poise and was smoothing her hair.

"Come on in and sit down. I'd like to introduce you to Cecilia and Ashley Melton," said Tessie.

"What a charming house," Julia said, looking around the living room. "Utterly charming." They had all trooped inside. Bear had gone to make some iced tea. The Melton family sat down stiffly, looking at each other as if they were strangers.

"First of all," Tessie said into the silence, "you ought to be very proud of Cecilia and Ashley Melton. They are two hard-working, decent people."

Julia looked bewildered. "Why what do you mean?" she asked cautiously, as if expecting a tease.

"I mean what I said," said Tessie.

"Oh." Julia smiled slightly. "Well, yes, of course. They are nice people. It's just that usually, you know, so often I get a somewhat different report of them."

"You mean HELP, take them away, brats, monsters. Right, Ashley?" Tessie laughed.

"Right," said Ashley. "Atrocious." He said this in a high voice, as if imitating a grand lady. For some reason, this imitation set them all to laughing.

Still catching his breath Tom became serious.

"What happened, Tessie?" he asked. "What on earth did you do to them?"

"We put them to work," Tessie said. "They took this ruined house and did some job on it."

"Now, Tessie," Julia protested. "I always gave Cecilia and Ashley jobs to do. But they simply refused."

"You'd forget and never check, anyway," said Ashley.

"I hate to nag people," Julia said. "I hate to pester and nag about things. I like the time I'm with the children to be pleasant."

"You never stopped us when we were terrible," Cecilia said sadly.

"You never did," Ashley repeated.

At this point Bear came back with a tray of iced tea.

"I've just had an idea," said Tom hesitantly. The idea seemed to be taking shape as he spoke and gazed at his two children. "I wonder how it would be if we, the four of us — Cecilia, Ashley, Mother, and I — took a little trip before school starts. You know, a week-long vacation. We could drive up to the Cape and stop at places near the beach and sightsee and swim."

Julia looked at Ashley and Cecilia. She still wore

a perplexed expression. "We could try it," she said. "Can you spare them, Tessie?"

"That would be okay, I guess," Tessie said grudgingly.

"We need them more than you do now, Tess," said Tom.

"I think it's a good idea," Ashley said. Cecilia agreed.

After that, Cecilia and Ashley showed their parents the work they had done. Ashley told about the Music Barn. Cecilia began to tell about the burglary and Sage and Lily Rose. Tom and Julia listened with rapt interest. The stories weren't half over when Tessie called them in to lunch.

Washing up for lunch, Cecilia looked at her reflection in the spotted mirror over the sink. She looked into the speckled green eyes that tilted slightly upward at the corners. She realized that they had just had a conversation, she and Tom and Julia and Ash, in which no one was trying to get something out of anyone. In which there had been no fits or tempers or insults. In which they had talked and listened and shared with pleasure. She turned off the tap and thought that perhaps the new Cecilia had a chance, even when this most surprising summer was over.